This book is dedicated to Toby, Leah, Addison, MKP and The Dude – they always Keep On Truckin'!

This edition
by Egmont
1 Nicholas
First printe
by Marvel

Cover pain
Special int
Art directe
Designed b

Copyright © 2017 MARVEL

MARVEL

ISBN 978 1 4052 8547 6
66850/1
Printed in Poland

Stay safe online. Egmont is not responsible
for content hosted by third parties.

MARVEL
GUARDIANS OF THE GALAXY

ROCKET AND GROOT

KEEP ON TRUCKIN'

by TOM ANGLEBERGER

After an epic battle with a
giant space thing that was
kind of like a squid but was
NOT a squid, our heroes
—ROCKET AND GROOT—
escaped Planet Shopping Mall
and were safe
in outer space ...
or so they thought ...

YOU HAVE TO READ THE FIRST BOOK!
ROCKET & GROOT: STRANDED ON PLANET SHOPPING MALL!

Instead they've run out of gas and are doomed to DIE a really BORING death …

unless their TAPE DISPENSER can save them!*

*It's a really really amazing purple tape dispenser!

CAPTAIN'S LOG
1

THE *RAKK 'N' RUIN* RUNS OUT OF GAS!*

Captain's Log!

This is
Captain Rocket
of the spaceship
Rakk 'n' Ruin!

← ME

I AM GROOT.

Right, Groot, it is **GREAT** to be off of that awful
shopping mall planet and back in our own spaceship!
Me and Groot are now headed back to Knowhere to
join the rest of the **Guardians of the Galaxy** and
get back to guarding the galaxy and stuff like that.

*Actually, Groot Smoothie – again, read the first book!

I AM GROOT.

Oh, yeah, you're right, Groot. I forgot to mention **Veronica**™, the totally **awesome**, **butt-kicking**, **super-intelligent tape dispenser**, who is also piloting the ship **AND** recording this **Captain's Log**. She's with us, too.

Heyyy!

(((•BING•))) I'M SORRY, YOUR CONTACT LIST HAS NO ENTRY FOR A **CAPTAIN SLOG**. WOULD YOU LIKE ME TO CHECK THE PHONE DIRECTORIES OF NEARBY PLANETS?

NO! Don't you start up with that again! You know I said Captain's **LOG**, not **Captain Slog!**

(((•BING•))) I'M SORRY, YOUR CONTACT LIST HAS NO ENTRY FOR A CAPTAIN SLOG. WOULD YOU LIKE ME TO CHECK THE PHONE DIRECTORIES OF NEARBY PLANETS?

NO!! I would like you to be quiet and let me draw the pictures to go with my Captain's Log.

(((•BING•))) I'M SORRY, YOUR CONTACT LIST HAS NO ENTRY FOR A CAPTAIN SLOG. WOULD YOU —

ARRRGGH!!! Just turn on your doodle app and let me draw!

(((•BING•))) LAUNCHING DOODLE APP.

sound of furry woodland creature
drawing on a touch screen with his
tiny little paws

NO! It would not be okay. I'm trying to concentrate here! Do you know how hard it is to draw **Groot's elbows?**

I AM GROOT?

Yes, that's **you!**

I AM GROOT!

Well, maybe I could draw better if you guys stopped interrupting me!

(((•BING•))) SO YOU DON'T WANT TO
BE INTERRUPTED?

EXACTLY!

((•BING•)) WHAT IF WE WERE ABOUT TO RUN OUT OF FUEL AND BECOME STRANDED IN THE COLD HEARTLESS VACUUM OF DEEP SPACE?

Okay, sure, if we were about to run out of fuel and become stranded in the heartless whatever, then, yes, it would be okay to interrupt me. Until then, **SHHHH!**

sound of 3.5 seconds of silence

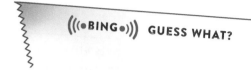 GUESS WHAT?

WHAT THE MONKEYBUTT IS IT NOW??????

I thought you weren't gonna interrupt me unless we were out of fuel ... and stranded in ... uh ... **OH, NO!!!!**

(((•BING•))) OH, YES.

WE'RE OUT OF FUEL?!?!?!?

(((•BING•))) YES.

But how can we be out of fuel?!?!? We just loaded up on a whole tankful of **Groot Smoothie** before we left the last planet!

sound of slurping

Oh, no! Groot? You haven't been drinking the Groot Smoothie, have you?

I ... AM GROOT.

Yes, you have! **We just heard you!**

sound of giant tree man letting out a spaceship-rattling belch

BURP

I knew it! First of all, that stuff is grosser than possum feet, second of all, it's loaded with preservatives, and third of all, **NOW WE'RE GOING TO BE STRANDED IN THE** — uh, what was it?

(((•BING•))) THE COLD HEARTLESS VACUUM OF DEEP SPACE.

THE COLD HEARTLESS VACUUM OF DEEP SPACE!

I AM GROOT...

It's too late for that now!
WE'RE ALL GONNA DIE!!!!

(((•BING•))) ACTUALLY, I WOULDN'T DIE, BECAUSE I'M A TAPE DISPENSER. AND TAPE DISPENSERS LIVE FOREVER.

Great ...

(((•BING•))) AND ACTUALLY, THERE'S A ONE-IN-A-MILLION CHANCE THAT YOU TWO WON'T DIE, EITHER. BUT IT REQUIRES IMMEDIATE ACTION.

I AM GROOT!

Yeah, whatever it is, **we'll do it!**

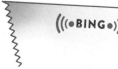

(((•BING•))) OKAY, THERE ARE TWO PLANETS THAT WE COULD POSSIBLY MAYBE GET TO IF WE ACT IMMEDIATELY.

**Yeah, yeah, you said that already!
Do it! Act immediately!**

(((•BING•))) FIRST WE HAVE TO DECIDE WHICH PLANET TO GO TO.

15

Fine, fine, what are they?

(((•BING•))) ONE IS BATTLETONIA, A PLANET THAT HAS BEEN FIGHTING A GLOBAL WAR FOR CENTURIES. IT'S FULL OF GUNS, BOMBS AND GUN BOMBS. ROCKET FUEL IS VERY SCARCE, AND WE'D HAVE TO FIGHT COUNTLESS BATTLES TO GET A TANKFUL.

Sounds great! **Let's go!!!**

I AM GROOT?

Okay, okay, what's the other planet?

(((•BING•))) THE OTHER PLANET IS HAPPYHAPPYFUNFUN, WHERE EVERYBODY IS PERFECTLY HAPPY AND THERE ARE NO WEAPONS AND NO WARS BUT PLENTY OF FREE ROCKET FUEL.

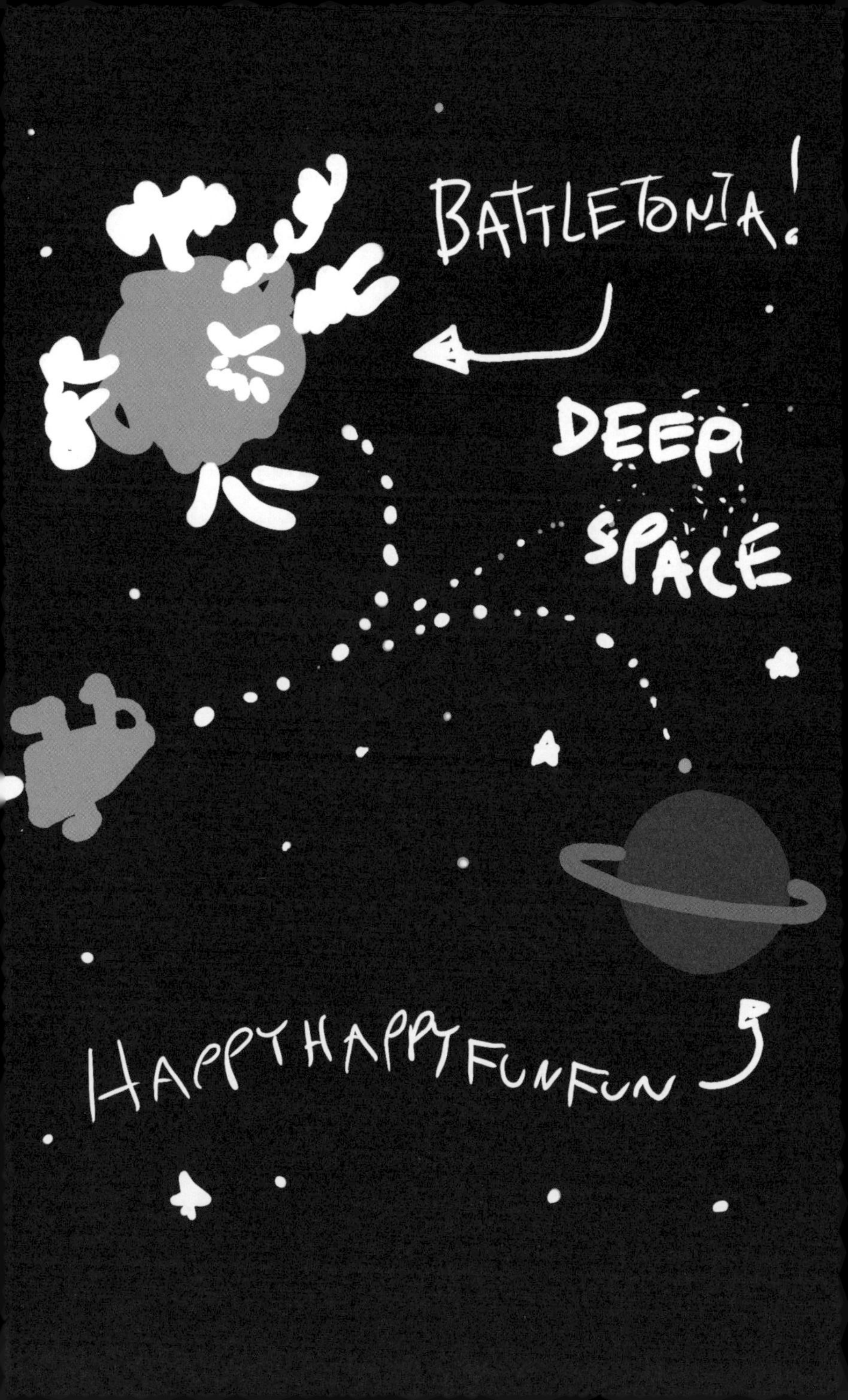
BATTLETONIA!
DEEP SPACE
HAPPYHAPPYFUNFUN

Okay, **BATTLETONIA** it is, then!

What? You've got to be kidding me.
All that happy-happy stuff would drive
me – uh, I mean **US** – insane!

What do you mean you've always dreamed
of relaxing on **a happy, peaceful planet?**
**You're one of the galaxy's
fiercest warriors!**

I AM GROOT.

WHAT???? How can you have a softer side? **You're a tree!**

 SORRY TO INTERRUPT, BUT WHILE YOU'VE BEEN ARGUING, WE'VE PASSED OUT OF RANGE OF BATTLETONIA.

So what are our options now?

 WE CAN EITHER GO TO HAPPYHAPPYFUNFUN OR DRIFT FOREVER IN THE COLD HEARTLESS VACUUM OF DEEP SPACE.

Whew! Man, this is a really tough decision.

Okay, okay, we can go to the happy place, but if anybody tries to hug me, **there's gonna be trouble!** I'm going to bring **my biggest rocket launcher,** and I'll have my finger on the trigger in case people look like they're going to break into song.

 UNFORTUNATELY, IT WILL NOT BE POSSIBLE FOR YOU TO BRING YOUR ROCKET LAUNCHER.

Okay, my plasma cannon. **Whatever.**

 UNFORTUNATELY, IT WILL NOT
BE POSSIBLE FOR YOU TO BRING
ANY WEAPONS.

WHY NOT?

(((•BING•))) BECAUSE IT TOOK YOU SO LONG TO MAKE A
DECISION, THERE IS NOW ONLY ONE WAY WE
CAN POSSIBLY REACH THE PLANET. WE HAVE
TO MAKE THE *RAKK 'N' RUIN* LIGHTER. SO I
HAVE EJECTED ALL WEAPONRY INTO SPACE.

NOOOOOO!

((•BING•)) I ALSO HAD TO EJECT ALL FOOD AND WATER, THE SEAT CUSHIONS, THE FUZZY DICE HANGING FROM THE REARVIEW MIRROR, THE TOILET SEAT, THE TOILET AND YOUR TAIL COMBS.

NOOOOOOOOOOOOOO!

((•BING•)) I WAS ABLE TO SAVE GROOT'S YO-YO, THOUGH.

I AM GROOT!

NOOOOOOOOO OOOOOOOO!

sound of furry woodland creature weeping

sound of giant tree man
playing with a yo-yo

sound of totally
awesome tape
dispenser setting
a course for
HappyHappyFunFun

CAPTAIN'S LOG
2

FUEL CRISIS

Captain's Log!

This is **Captain Rocket** of the spaceship **_Rakk 'n' Ruin_** in orbit around the planet – ugh – **HappyHappyFunFun.**

ME BEING ANGRY

I want to make one thing perfectly clear before I begin this Captain's Log.

(((•BING•))) I'M SORRY, YOUR CONTACT LIST —

THE THING ... I want to make clear is that even though I am speaking out loud and Veronica™ is recording me, **I am not actually speaking to Veronica™. I am mad at Veronica™. I am furious with Veronica™. I am –**

I AM GROOT.

Yes, Groot, I know that she **saved our lives** by figuring how to get us out of the heartless whatever of deep space and get us to this planet. But it is the **WRONG** planet and she threw away **all of our guns and cannons and kaboomulators** to get us here.

I AM GROOT.

Dude, we are **Guardians of the Galaxy!** How are we supposed to go around Guardianalyzing stuff without the proper weapons?

That reminds me! We've got to let
Star-Lord know that we're gonna be late.
Veronica™, can you send a message to —

((●BING●)) I THOUGHT YOU WEREN'T TALKING TO ME.

Oh, forget that —

((●BING●)) MAYBE I'M NOT TALKING TO **YOU** NOW!

You ARE talking to me!

((●BING●)) ...

Grrr!

((●BING●)) !

GRRRRR!

((•BING•)) !!!!!!!!!!!

GRRRRRRRRRRR!!!!!

I AM GROOT!

((•BING•)) THE GIANT TREE MAN IS RIGHT.

Yes ... sniff ... he sure is!

((•BING•)) WOULD YOU LIKE A HUG?

NO! But I would like you to send that **message to Star-Lord!**

((•BING•)) SORRY, BUT THE INTERGALACTIC WI-FI CHANNELS ARE CURRENTLY BUSY DOWNLOADING AN UPGRADE TO THE DOODLE APP.

Well, cancel that! **This is important!!!**

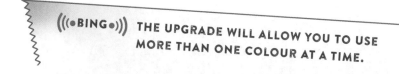

((•BING•)) THE UPGRADE WILL ALLOW YOU TO USE MORE THAN ONE COLOUR AT A TIME.

Sweet hamsters! It's about time! Forget Star-Lord and get me that upgrade!

sound of time passing

((•BING•)) DOWNLOAD COMPLETE!

HOLY UNICORN TOEJAM! LOOK AT ALL THE PRETTY COLOURS!

(((●BING●))) WE ARE IN ORBIT AROUND PLANET HAPPYHAPPYFUNFUN. SHOULD I SEND THAT MESSAGE TO STAR-LORD NOW?

No, first I want you to call down to the spaceport and have them get a truckload of rocket fuel ready for us. **I want to gas and go!**

I AM GROOT?

What? No, there won't be time for any shopping! And anyway, we just left an endless shopping mall. What could you possibly need?

I AM GROOT...

Oh, your **yo-yo string** broke ... Okay, Veronica™, have them send over a truckload of rocket fuel **AND** some string.

 GAS AND YO-YO STRING ORDERS HAVE BEEN PLACED.

(((•BING•))) BEGINNING LANDING PROCEDURE.

sound of expertly piloted
spaceship using its last drop of
fuel to make a perfect landing

sound of furry woodland
creature and giant tree man ignoring perfect
landing because they are playing with the
new doodle app

(((•BING•))) WE'RE HERE ...

(((•BING•))) HELLOOOOOOOO ...?

(((•BING•))) I'VE SAVED YOUR LIVES.

(((•BING•))) AGAIN.

Great, thanks. Hey, look at how much better
I look in **brown!**

(((•BING•))) WHEE ... DID I MENTION THAT
WE'RE HERE?

Okay, okay, this is **Captain Rocket** about to step through the airlock onto the planet HappyHappyFunFun to make sure the gas tank gets **filled all the way.**

((•BING•)) OPENING AIRLOCK.

I AM GROOT...

No, the airlock isn't smaller! You just got chubby from drinking all that **Groot Smoothie!** Here, I'll give you a push ...

sound of giant tree man squeezing out of airlock

sound of giant tree man, furry woodland
creature and totally awesome tape dispenser
descending the ramp to the planet's surface

This is one small step for —

I AM GROOT.

Oh, right ... Here comes the fuel truck.

sound of truck engine

Gee, they're driving pretty fast. I guess they're really in a hurry to help us out.

sound of truck engine getting louder

Seems like maybe they should be **slowing** down now ...

sound of truck engine roaring

It almost looks like he's gonna run us over ... but something like that would **never** happen on a happy, fun planet like **HappyHappyFunFun!**

sound of truck engine revving even louder

Would it?

((•BING•)) ONE SECOND TO IMPACT!

HOLY MOLE NOSTRILS!
We're gonna be roadkill!

I AM GROOT!!!!

sound of giant tree man
grabbing furry woodland creature and totally
awesome tape dispenser and leaping
to the side just in time

Well, that was neither happy nor fun!!!

sound of truck making a
tire-screeching U-turn

It's coming back to try again!

(((•BING•))) ANOTHER TRUCK IS APPROACHING
AT HIGH SPEED!

What? Did you order **two** trucks of gas?

(((•BING•))) NO, THIS IS THE YO-YO STRING
DELIVERY TRUCK!

I AM GROOT!

No, Groot, I didn't know that yo-yo strings are
coated with highly explosive yo-yo wax. But what
does that have to do with ... Oh, no ...

sound of both trucks revving their engines

(((•BING •))) DO YOU KNOW THE ODDS OF SURVIVING A HEAD-ON COLLISION BETWEEN A ROCKET-FUEL TANKER AND A YO-YO STRING TRUCK?

Never tell me the odds!

(((•BING •))) ACTUALLY, I WASN'T GOING TO TELL YOU THE ODDS. I WAS WONDERING IF YOU KNEW, BECAUSE I CAN'T FIGURE OUT WHICH FORMULA TO USE.

The answer's gonna be ZERO unless we can get back on the ship ... FAST!!!

sound of engines roaring

sound of giant tree man lunging up the ramp and squeezing back through the airlock while holding furry woodland creature and totally awesome tape dispenser

sound of airlock door slamming
milliseconds before –

sound of trucks crashing,
atoms smashing, fuel splashing,
yo-yo strings igniting and
the whole spaceport going
KABOOMABOOBOO!

43

CAPTAIN'S LOG

3

AIRBORNE

Captain's Log.

This is **Captain Rocket** back on the *Rakk 'n' Ruin*.
We just got blown sky – **oof!** – high by that
explosion! Now we're – **OUCH!**

> sound of furry woodland creature
> and giant tree man smashing into the floor,
> walls and ceiling as the ship tumbles
> helplessly through the air

Groot, you just landed on my – **OUCH!!!**
You did it again!!!!!!!!

I AM GROO—OOF!

I accept your — **YOWCH!!!!!**

 BETTER LET ME TAPE YOU BOYS TO THE FLOOR, BECAUSE WE ARE GOING TO BE LANDING IN ABOUT FIVE SECONDS.

(((●BING●))) AND WHEN I SAY 'LANDING', I REALLY MEAN 'FALLING OUT OF THE SKY AND CRASHING INTO THE DOWNTOWN AREA OF A VAST AND BUSY CITY'.

Well, as long as it ain't another shopping mall,
I don't care where we crash-land, but yeah,
maybe a little tape to cushion the landing.

**sound of totally awesome tape dispenser
totally saving the lives of furry woodland
creature and giant tree man through the
power of her mighty adhesives**

**sound of spaceship crashing into
the downtown area of a vast
and busy city**

**sound of spaceship going through
the roof of a combination dance
and karate school**

Well, at least we don't hafta find a parking spot.
Let's go look around ...

sound of airlock opening

This is **Captain Rocket**. We are about to exit the
Rakk 'n' Ruin and explore this big, big, busy city.
By the way, Veronica™, do you know the name of
this place?

(((•BING•))) YES.

Well, **what is it?!?**

(((•BING•))) YOU'RE NOT GOING TO LIKE IT!

Just **tell me!**

(((•BING•))) HUGGSBURG.

sound of furry woodland creature groaning

sound of furry woodland creature,
giant tree man and totally awesome
tape dispenser going through the airlock

I don't believe it! We've crash-landed in **Debbie-Don's Dance Dojo**! Good thing Debbie-Don wasn't here! She'd be furious! Hey, look! I can get a new sweatshirt to replace my old one, which got soaked in space-squid sewage.

OLD

SPACE SQUID SEWAGE

NEW

How do you like this blue one?

 YOU LOOK HOT!

Say wha???

 I'M CONCERNED THIS PLANET MAY BE TOO WARM FOR SWEATSHIRT WEARING.

Oh ... well, I'm not going around naked!

I AM GROOT!

I don't care if you're comfortable walking around with no clothes on. **I'm NOT!**

sound of zipper zipping

Hey, what's that noise?

((•BING•)) YOU MEAN THE ZIPPER ZIPPING?

No, I mean that **vroom-vroom** sound.

sound of vroom-vroom

 **MY SENSORS INDICATE THAT IT'S TWENTY-SEVEN MINIVANS DRIVING AT TOP SPEED TOWARDS THIS BUILDING.**

Hmmm. Maybe it's time for ballet class?

sound of twenty-seven
building-shaking crashes

Holy chipmunk cheeks! They're crashing right into the front of the Dance Dojo! Debbie-Don is REALLY gonna be furious!

sound of many more
building-shaking crashes

Sweet gopher goiters! There are more of them crashing into the back!! They're tearing the building apart!

$(((\bullet BING\bullet)))$ MY SENSORS INDICATE THE WALLS WILL CRUMBLE IN THIRTY SECONDS. FOLLOWED THREE SECONDS LATER BY US BEING RUN OVER BY WHICHEVER MINIVANS ARE STILL RUNNING.

I AM GROOT!

Right, pal! **Let's get out of here!** Can you lift us through the hole in the roof?

sound of giant tree man lifting
furry woodland creature and totally awesome
tape dispenser through the hole in the roof
made by the *Rakk 'n' Ruin*

sound of giant tree man climbing
out through the hole in the roof

sound of an army of minivans
racing in from every direction

(((•BING•))) MY BUILT-IN RADAR SHOWS SEVERAL
THOUSAND ADDITIONAL MINIVANS
HEADED THIS WAY!

I AM GROOT?!?!?

No, buddy, I don't know why every soccer mom on the planet would be after us!

Moms LOVE me!

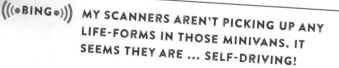 MY SCANNERS AREN'T PICKING UP ANY LIFE-FORMS IN THOSE MINIVANS. IT SEEMS THEY ARE ... SELF-DRIVING!

I AM GROOT?!?!?

Self-driving.

It means they can drive by themselves!

I AM GROOT?

No, buddy, I don't know why every self-driving
minivan on the planet would be after us!

Self-driving minivans
LOVE me, too!

sound of walls breaking
and roof shaking

We've got to get
off this roof!
FAST!!!

CAPTAIN'S LOG

4

A DANGEROUS CROSSING

Captain's Log.

This is **Captain Rocket!** We're in **big trouble!**
We're trapped on the roof of a building that
self-driving minivans are smashing to bits!

(((•BING•))) ESTIMATED TIME UNTIL BUILDING
COLLAPSE IS — OH, WAIT, NEVER MIND.

WHAT IS IT?

(((•BING•))) YOU DON'T WANT TO KNOW!

You're right! I **don't!** Okay, we've got to get to that next building without touching the ground where the minivans will run us over! But it's WAY too far to jump! Any ideas?

You're going to make a bridge out of your body for us? Dude, that is **sweet,** but it's too far. You'll never reach it!

I AM GROOT...

**sound of giant tree man's
legs growing longer**

Oh, yeah, I always forget you can do that! That should do it. Now just lay down across the gap and —

(((•BING•))) THE CORRECT GRAMMAR IS 'LIE DOWN'.

Do you want me to carry you across or not?

sound of building collapsing

(((•BING•))) 'LAY DOWN' IS FINE! JUST FINE! IN FACT, IT HAS A MORE NATURAL FEEL TO IT! I LOVE IT! LET'S GO!

sound of furry woodland creature
scampering across giant-tree-man
bridge towards safety

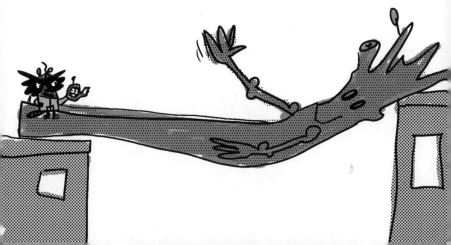

Great weasel whiskers!

What is that minivan doing?

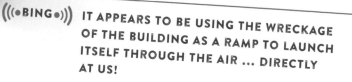 IT APPEARS TO BE USING THE WRECKAGE OF THE BUILDING AS A RAMP TO LAUNCH ITSELF THROUGH THE AIR ... DIRECTLY AT US!

sound of minivan hitting ramp
and catching big air

I CAN'T LOOK!

(((•BING•))) I CAN'T LOOK!

I AM GROOT!!

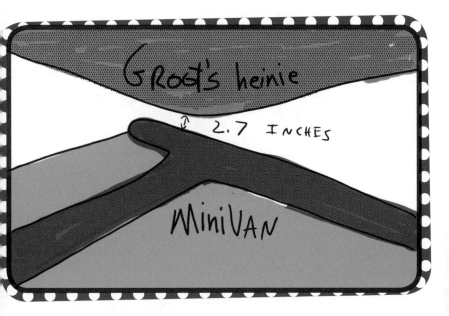

sound of minivan passing just 2.7 inches below Groot's wooden heinie

(((•BING•))) HERE COMES ANOTHER ONE AND IT'S GOING OFF A BIGGER RAMP! MY CALCULATIONS SAY IT'S GOING TO JUMP THREE INCHES HIGHER THAN THE LAST ONE! IT'S GOING TO HIT US!

Groot! We've only got one chance!

CLENCH YOUR BUM!

CLENCH!!!!

sound of giant tree man clenching his bum

 (((•BING•))) IT'S NOT ENOUGH! BRACE FOR IMPACT!

sound of minivan hitting ramp and catching slightly bigger air

Clench, Groot, clench!!!

For the love of capybaras,

CLENCH!

I...AM...
GROOOOOOOOOT...

sound of giant tree man clenching his
bark bum just a little more

sound of minivan passing just 0.2 inches
below Groot's clenched wooden heinie

You did it, buddy! Great clenching!!

(((•BING•))) QUICK! SCAMPER THE REST OF THE WAY!

I never scamper.

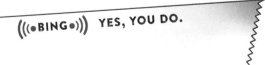 **(((•BING•)))** YES, YOU DO.

NO, I **don't!**

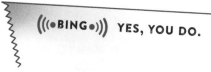 **(((•BING•)))** YES, YOU DO.

NO, I **d—uh-oh.**

**sound of two minivans jumping off the
two ramps at the same time**

Why in the naked mole rat are they doing that?
Don't they know they're just going to miss again?

 **(((•BING•)))** MY CALCULATIONS SHOW THEM HITTING
EACH OTHER HEAD-ON IN A FIERY
EXPLOSION DIRECTLY BELOW US!

It's **scampering time!!!**

**sound of furry woodland creature
scampering across giant-tree-man bridge**

Quick, Groot ... Uh, wait ... How was he supposed to get himself over here without touching the ground?

I AM GROOT...?

Give me a second to think!

(((•BING•))) SORRY, THE HEAD-ON COLLISION WILL OCCUR IN LESS THAN ONE SECOND!

NOOOOOOOOOOO!

sound of explosion cracking Groot in two

NOOO OOOOOOO OOOOOOOOOO!

sound of Groot's top half flipping
through the air and landing on the roof
next to furry woodland creature

YES!!!!

sound of woodland creature
hugging giant tree man

By the rings of my tail, I thought I'd lost you, buddy!

sound of tape dispenser wiggling tape affectionately

((•BING•)) I AM GLAD YOU ARE NOT DEAD.

I AM GROOT!

LOOK! Your legs have landed in the rubble of the old building! They are doing a little dance! It appears to be the rhumba!

I AM GROOT!

Well, whatever it is, it's distracting the minivans! They're all trying to run over your old legs, but the legs are too fast! Holy lemur lint, I've never seen anything like it!

(((•BING•))) PERHAPS INSTEAD OF WATCHING GROOT'S LEGS GETTING FUNKY, WE SHOULD MAKE USE OF THE DISTRACTION AND ESCAPE UNNOTICED.

Right! We just need to get off this roof and inside the building.

sound of top half of giant tree man
punching a hole in the roof

sound of top half of giant tree man,
furry woodland creature and totally
awesome undamaged tape dispenser
dropping through the hole into some
unknown but strangely familiar store

I AM GROOT!

You're right, buddy, this unknown store is strangely familiar ...

Hello, Valued Customers! Welcome to H. F. Happy Tooth's High-Fructose World!

CAPTAIN'S LOG

5

AN OLD FRIEND

Captain's Log!

This is **Captain Rocket!** We are under attack by
H. F. Happy Tooth and his army of killer robo-tooth
fairies! Veronica™! Groot! **Prepare for battle!!!!!**

If you're looking
for anything in
particular, just
ask, and I'll help
you find it.

What the tail hair?
Why isn't he trying to **kill** us?

(((●BING●))) REMEMBER ... THIS ISN'T THE SAME H. F. HAPPY TOOTH WE FOUGHT ON THE LAST PLANET.*

(((●BING●))) *READ *ROCKET AND GROOT: STRANDED ON PLANET SHOPPING MALL* FOR THE FULL STORY OF OUR BATTLE WITH H. F. HAPPY TOOTH AND HIS ROBO-FAIRIES. SPOILER ALERT: I WAS TOTALLY AWESOME IN THAT ONE.

THERE'S MORE THAN ONE HAPPY TOOTH?

Veronica™! Groot! Prepare for the battle of our lives!!!!

We're having a sale on Twizzlers.

Huh?

(((●BING●))) BASED ON MY SPECIES CALCULATOR, THERE ARE HAPPY TOOTH ROBOTS ALL OVER THE GALAXY. THE ONE WE MET BEFORE HAD BEEN PROGRAMMED TO KILL US. THIS ONE JUST WANTS US TO BUY SOMETHING.

Oh ...

I AM GROOT!

Sorry, Groot, we **can't** buy anything!
We still don't have any **money**!

I AM GROOT!!

H.F. Happytooth's Clip'N'Slurp COUPON

Bring this coupon to ANY H _____ oth's location for a FREE* bucke _____ r highest fructose corn syrup with _____ YOUR CHOICE of over three s _____ flavors! Clip 'N' Slurp TODAY!
*Void on planets where high-fructos _____ corn syrup is classified as toxic wast _____

You have a **coupon**? Where'd you get that?

From the last planet?? Do you mean that while Veronica™ and I were **fighting for our lives** against killer robots, you were **clipping a coupon** to save a few cents off some **candy?**

Oh, the coupon is for **free candy?** Well, fine, then, go ahead.

sound of giant tree man giving
tooth robot a coupon

Oh, yay. This coupon entitles you to a free bucket of high-fructose corn syrup with sprinkles.

sound of tooth robot pushing button on syrup machine

Hey, everybody!!! It's me, Bobby Sprinkles Jr.!!!!!

Hey, Bobby. We've got customers ... sorta.

Customers?!?!? Does someone actually want my syrup??? Oh, boy! Howdy, Valued Customers, I'm Bobby Sprinkles Jr.! I'd like to extrude some corn syrup for you and then sprinkle on some—

Actually, they're just using a coupon.

Oh, too bad ... Oh, well, anyway, here's your syrup.

sound of syrup machine squirting a
stream of icky, sticky syrup into bucket

(((•BING•))) THANKS, BOBBY SPRINKLES! YOU DO THAT
REALLY WELL!

Aw, thanks! Hey, my sensors indicate
that you're a totally awesome tape
dispenser!

sound of tape dispenser blushing

Geez, this guy is worse than Star-Lord! Would you
stop flirting with our tape dispenser and give us our
monkey-lovin' sprinkles?!

I'm sorry. I do not have the flavour monkey-lovin'. I have lime, cherry, lemon or dirt-flavoured sprinkles!!! They're all GREAT! Plus, they're all guaranteed to probably not give you diarrhoea!*

I AM GROOT.

What? Not dirt flavour again! Why do you always have to pick **dirt** flavour?

I AM GROOT!

sound of furry woodland creature pouting like a baby

sound of syrup machine sprinkling sprinkles in bucket

*Warning: May cause diarrhoea.

Here you go, Valued Customers!

sound of slurping

sound of giant tree man growing legs

I AM GROOT!

Glad you liked it, Valued Customers! Even though you were just using a coupon, I still hope you have a sprinkle-tastic day!!!! I mean that!

(((●BING●))) AND YOU HAVE A SPRINKLE-TASTIC DAY, TOO, BOBBY!!!

All right, all right, just give me the coupon and get outta my store!

Gee, Mr. Happy Tooth, you don't seem as **happy** as the last tooth robot we saw. Whenever they weren't trying to kill us, he and his robo-tooth fairies kept singing songs.

You want a song, Valued Customer? Okay ...

**sound of tooth robot getting
out a beat-up guitar**

**sound of a robo-tooth fairy
playing the harmonica**

**sound of tooth robot singing
with heartbreaking tenderness**

They call me Mr. Happy Tooth,

But if you wanna know the truth ...

The blues done come around.

And my cavity-riddled smile is now a frown ...

It's now a frown ... It's upside down ...

I don't get it! How can a customer service robot
get the blues?

Cause I-I-I-I-I-I-I-I-I ain't got no customers ...

He-e-e-e-e-e-e ain't got no customers ... no Val-ued Customers ...

Yeah ... where are the customers? We haven't seen any people since we landed on this planet.

Yo, the groundhog wants to know

Where did they go?

Where did they go?

Where did they [beatboxing]
goooooooooo ... oooooooo ...
oooooooooooooooooo ... oooooooo?

They went down, down, down, doobie down, doo-doo down.

Down undergrouuuuuund.

Underground? What are they doing underground?

I don't know, but they sure aren't buying Twizzlers anymore! Do you know how many Twizzlers we have in the back room? And don't even get me started about the Reese's Pieces ...

(((•BING•))) JUST A MINUTE! I'M RECEIVING A VIDEO PHONE CALL THAT MAY HELP US UNDERSTAND WHAT'S GOING ON.

Who is it?

(((•BING•))) THE PRESIDENT OF THE PLANET, DINA THE WONDER LIZARD.

CAPTAIN'S LOG
6

TALKING TO THE PLANETARY PRESIDENT

Captain's Log.

Captain Rocket here, of the spaceship
Rakk 'n' Ruin. This is Groot and Veronica™.

Hello, Captain Rocket, Groot and Veronica™. I'm Dina the Wonder Lizard, the president of this planet. Hope you don't mind me calling! I got your number from Star-Lord.

((•BING•)) IT'S AN HONOUR, PRESIDENT WONDER LIZARD!

Please, call me President Dee-Dee. We're less formal now that we're living in holes in the ground.

That's what we want to know! **WHY** are you living in holes in the ground?

Have you SEEN any cars or trucks since you landed?

SEEN THEM? They've almost killed us three times!

Well, that's why we're living underground.
THEY TRIED TO KILL US, TOO.

WHY?

BEFORE

AFTER

WE DON'T KNOW. UP UNTIL TWO MONTHS AGO, WE HAD A **PERFECT PLANET**.
PERFECT CITIES, **PERFECT** CITIZENS, LOTS OF HUGGING ... EVERYTHING WAS
PERFECT! WELL, EXCEPT FOR OUR TV SHOWS. OUR TV SHOWS WERE ALL ABOUT
PERFECT PEOPLE BEHAVING PERFECTLY, AND THAT WAS SOOOO BORING. LIKE,
THERE WAS THIS ONE TV SHOW ABOUT A BOY LIZARD-LIKE ALIEN WHO GOT A
JOB AT A RESTAURANT WHERE THIS GIRL LIZARD-LIKE ALIEN WAS A KLUTZY
WAITRESS, BUT REALLY SHE WAS A MOVIE STAR PRETENDING TO BE A KLUTZY
WAITRESS, BUT THE FIRST LIZARD-LIKE ALIEN, WHO REALLY WAS A KLUTZY
WAITER, FELL IN LOVE WITH HER AND THEN WHEN —

Excuse me, President Dee-Dee, could we get back to the part about why the cars are trying to kill us?

Oh, yeah, right. See, they used to be **PERFECT**, too! Driving us wherever we wanted to go, making deliveries, picking up garbage ... all without a single accident. They were **PERFECT** drivers! Then, suddenly, something went wrong with the central computer that controls the whole system! And you've seen the results! MOTORIZED MAYHEM!

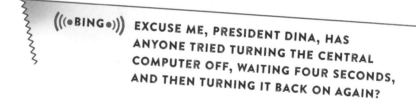 EXCUSE ME, PRESIDENT DINA, HAS ANYONE TRIED TURNING THE CENTRAL COMPUTER OFF, WAITING FOUR SECONDS, AND THEN TURNING IT BACK ON AGAIN?

No one can get near it! The central computer used to be called Safe-T-Drive3000. But now it calls itself

BIG MAMA AND IT SENDS OUT KILLER TRUCKS TO DESTROY ANYONE WHO COMES ANYWHERE NEAR ITS ISLAND FORTRESS.

What if you —

Excuse me one moment. My vice president is here with an URGENT message for me.

President Dee-Dee! It's your daughter!!!
She's missing!!!!

Oh, no, my sweet baby!!! If she's gone up to the surface, she's in TERRIBLE DANGER!!!!!!!!!!!!!!!!!!

 PRESIDENT DINA, IS YOUR DAUGHTER A LIZARD-LIKE ALIEN LIKE YOU, BUT SHORTER AND CUTE AS A BUTTON?

Yes, but why?

 BECAUSE SHE'S IN THE MIDDLE OF THE ROAD IN FRONT OF THE STORE RIGHT NOW AND ABOUT TO BE RUN OVER BY A GLUTEN-FREE VANILLA WAFER DELIVERY TRUCK!

CAPTAIN'S LOG

7

DELIVERANCE

This is **Captain Rocket** ... I don't have time for the Captain's Log right now! But if I die in the next thirty seconds, I want to make it clear that Star-Lord is not welcome to sing at my funeral. If Drax wants to sing, that's fine, but **NOT** Star-Lord. **NO way!**

sound of gluten-free vanilla wafer
delivery truck getting even closer to cute,
helpless lizard-like alien child

Okay, Veronica™ ... **gimme some tape!**

(((•BING•))) HOW MUCH TAPE DO YOU NEED?

Just let it roll, and then get ready to reel me back in.

Trust me, you'll
approve ...

sound of totally awesome
tape dispenser dispensing tape

sound of furry woodland creature wrapping
end of tape around his ringed tail

sound of cute, helpless lizard-like alien
child screaming in terror as gluten-free
vanilla wafer delivery truck speeds up

Throw me, Groot!

I AM GROOT!

sound of giant tree man picking up
furry woodland creature and throwing
him at store window

sound of store window shattering

sound of furry woodland creature
bursting through shattered glass, then
bouncing and skidding across road

sound of furry woodland creature hugging cute, helpless lizard-like alien child – AWWW!

REEL ME IN, Veronica™!!!!!

sound of totally awesome tape dispenser reeling in the tape, which is tied to the furry woodland creature, who is hugging the cute, helpless lizard-like alien child–AWWWW! SO CUTE!

sound of gluten-free vanilla wafer delivery truck roaring past just milliseconds later

Well, President Dina, here's your child!

Me waNT CANDY!

Oh, Bertha, you NAUGHTY child! You must never go to the surface again! Mommy will order you candy next time.

Me waNT CANDY! Me waNT Gummy bear! Is ThaT Gummy bear? Yum!

sound of cute lizard-like alien child
biting furry woodland creature

YOWCH!

GGRRR

Don't worry, she probably didn't use her POISON GLANDS.

PROBABLY???

Oh, Captain Rocket, thank you so much for saving her! I'd like to give you a REWARD!

Great, how about some

rocket fuel!

I'd be glad to ... but there's no way to deliver it to your ship, because of the CENTRAL COMPUTER and all of those INSANE vehicles.

Okay, then how about some rocket launchers, some plasma blasters and a box of photon grenades so we can go blow up the central computer!

HappyHappyFunFun is – or was – a PEACEFUL planet.
THERE ARE NO WEAPONS OF ANY KIND.

NOOOO OOOOOOO!!!!!!!

Excuse me, President Dina ... your child just drank a bucket of high-fructose corn syrup and is now beating my robot tooth fairies over the heads with an all-day sucker.

ISN'T SHE PRECIOUS? YOU DON'T MIND RAISING HER THERE IN THE CANDY STORE, DO YOU? I'M AFRAID TO LEAVE THIS CAVE TO COME GET HER. LET HER EAT ALL THE CANDY SHE WANTS AND CHARGE IT TO MY ACCOUNT.

Robo-fairies! We finally have a customer!!! And ... someone to love!

Activating HUG Mode!

We have **GOT** to get out of here!!!!!

CAPTAIN'S LOG

8

UP-TEMPO MUSIC MONTAGE

Captain's Log.

This is **Captain Rocket**. Me and the rest of the crew are trapped in a candy store with a bunch of huggy tooth fairies and an **adorable** lizard child.

 (((•BING•))) THE ADORABLE LIZARD CHILD IS DROOLING ON ME. THAT IS NOT AN APPROVED USE.

Somehow we've got to get **out of here** and get to that central computer. Hey, Veronica™, how far is it to the central computer's ... uh ... computer centre?

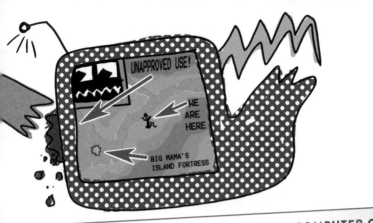

((•BING•))) THE CENTRAL COMPUTER'S COMPUTER CENTRE IS LOCATED ON A SMALL ISLAND ON THE OTHER SIDE OF HUGGSBURG. IT'S ABOUT TWENTY MILES AWAY. ALSO, THE ADORABLE LIZARD CHILD JUST PUT A PEANUT BUTTER CUP INTO MY DISK DRIVE!

THAT IS NOT AN APPROVED USE!!!!

Uh-huh, right. So there's **no way** we can walk twenty miles with all those crazy cars out there. In fact, we couldn't walk twenty feet! What we need is our own **crazy** car!

I AM GROOT?

I'm glad you asked, buddy! We're gonna **make** one!

I AM GROOT?

Sure, I know how to make a car!
I think. First we need like
a big metal container of some
sort that we can all sit in. Hey,
Happy Tooth, you got
a dumpster out back?

Yes, back when we had customers, we used to throw out candy wrappers, empty sugar buckets, cavity-filled teeth, etc ...

Great! Mind if we borrow it?

Dude, if you can fix these cars and get my customers back, you can borrow anything you want.

I'm glad you said that, 'cause I'm gonna need Bobby Sprinkles, too.

Is that okay with you, Bobby Sprinkles?

If it means spending more time with this wonderful tape dispenser, then it's a big

YES!

Would you **stop** it before I barf up a crayfish?

sound of tape dispenser sticking out tongue at furry woodland creature

Okay ... Groot, this is going to take incredible **physical strength!**

I AM GROOT!

And, Veronica™, it's gonna take **a lot** of tape!

((•BING•)) HOW MUCH TAPE DO YOU NEED?

I just said ... **A LOT!** Okay, folks, let's get to work! We got a vehicle to build.

((•BING•)) I'VE NOTICED THAT IN POPULAR MOVIES AND TV SHOWS, MOMENTS LIKE THIS OFTEN HAVE AN UP-TEMPO ROCK-AND-ROLL SONG!

Yeah, **Happy Tooth**, why don't you and the tooth fairies play something?

I got them blues...

Dude, we were looking for something a little more **punk rock.**

sound of Happy Tooth and robo-fairies
ripping into insane, hard-core, totally
boss heavy metal version of
'Hey, Sweetie, How About
Some Sugar?'

sound of giant tree man
lifting dumpster in air

sound of furry woodland creature
positioning Bobby Sprinkles' nozzles and
sprinkle shakers under dumpster

sound of totally awesome tape dispenser
taping nozzles and shakers in place

sound of cute lizard-like alien child
going poo-poo in her diaper

sound of Happy Tooth and robo-fairies
hitting the final note just as furry
woodland creature finishes work
on the dumpster car

CAPTAIN'S LOG

THE *FASTTRASH3000*

Captain's Log.

This is **Captain Rocket**, pilot of the land vehicle *FastTrash3000*.

Groot, Veronica™ and I have boarded the *FastTrash3000* and are about to **try it out.**

Everybody ready? Okay, **let's slide!**

I AM GROOT?

Right, see, we didn't have anything to make **wheels** with. So the *FastTrash3000* sprays a thin mist of corn syrup in front of us and we just glide and slide down the highway.

I AM GROOP

It works like this. See, I **step** on this Hershey's bar with almonds, which **pulls** on this extra-long Twizzler, which **turns** on Bobby Sprinkles' sprinkle sprinklers, which I've converted into **turbo-powered sprinkle jets.**

sound of furry woodland creature stepping on Hershey's bar with almonds sound of sprinkle jets firing!

sound of the *FastTrash3000* slowly
building speed, then racing down the alley

YEE-HAW!

(((•BING•))) **YEE-HAW!**

I AM
GROOOOOOOOOT!

I've never felt so **alive!**

 **HOW DO YOU STEER? JUST ASKING.**

Hmmm, I hadn't thought that through yet.

 **NO BIGGIE. JUST ASKING BECAUSE WE'VE JUST LEFT THE ALLEY AND ARE HEADED THE WRONG WAY DOWN A ONE-WAY STREET AND ARE ABOUT TO CRASH HEAD-ON INTO A SEÑOR SAVE-A-LOT-BRAND REFRIED BEAN TRUCK!**

Okay, let me think for a minute!

 **WE DON'T HAVE A MINUTE. IMPACT WITH REFRIED BEAN TRUCK IN FIVE SECONDS!**

Five seconds? Flaming walrus moustaches! **We're gonna die!**

Die? But I just started living! Oh! The years I wasted in that candy shop! And now after a brief taste of freedom – and love – it's all over!!

(((•BING•))) ACTUALLY, THE FURRY WOODLAND CREATURE SAYS STUFF LIKE THAT ALL THE TIME. THEN SOMETHING CRAZY HAPPENS AND WE DON'T DIE.

I AM GROOT!

sound of giant tree man growing extra-large head

sound of giant tree man head-butting
refried bean delivery truck

(((•BING•))) SEE WHAT I MEAN, BOBBY?

sound of refried beans
going everywhere

Thanks, Groot!

Sorry I panicked. I've always had a fear of refried beans. You see, when I was just a child, there was a –

(((•BING•))) SORRY TO INTERRUPT, BUT THERE ARE MANY MORE VEHICLES HEADED TOWARDS US AND WE STILL DON'T HAVE A WAY TO STEER.

No problem! I'll just rig up a couple of these gummy snakes and attach one end to the sprinkle shooters and the other end to these gummy lips. You put on the gummy lips and then lean left or right to steer. Who wants to go first?

sound of awkward silence

(((•BING•))) WELL, SOMEBODY BETTER DO SOMETHING, BECAUSE HERE COMES A DIAPER DELIVERY TRUCK!!!

I AM GROOT!

No, Groot! Don't destroy it! I think it's headed for Happy Tooth's! That adorable lizard child definitely needed a fresh diaper. I'll try steering around it.

sound of furry woodland creature
putting on gummy lips, then leaning right

sound of the *FastTrash3000* swerving
left, barely missing the diaper truck
and making an illegal left turn onto
West Lizardo Street

Whoa! I think I hooked up these gummy snakes wrong! It's really hard to steer this thing!

(((●BING●))) WEST LIZARDO STREET IS THE CURVIEST STREET IN NEW FUN CITY.

(((●BING●))) ALSO THE STEEPEST.

(((●BING●))) AND WE'RE GOING DOWNHILL.

I AM GROOT?

Brakes? Brakes are for wimps.

Just hold on!

sound of furry woodland creature using
gummy lips to steer the *FastTrash3000*
downhill, around curves, through a
burrito-to-go restaurant, over a lawn gnome,
into and out of a fountain, and finally, through
a red light and down the middle of a freeway

I think I'm getting the hang of this!

 **(((•BING•)))** GOOD! BECAUSE HERE COMES A GIANT GARBAGE TRUCK! IMPACT IN FIVE SECONDS!

YEE-HAW!

It'll have to catch us first!

sound of the *FastTrash3000*
hanging a U-turn!

sound of garbage truck speeding up

(((•BING•))) IT'S GAINING ON US.

Oh, yeah? **Watch this!**

sound of the *FastTrash3000* crashing
over the edge of a bridge and landing on
West Gecko Avenue

sound of garbage truck crashing
over the edge of a bridge and landing on
West Gecko Avenue

(((•BING•))) IT'S CATCHING US!

Mangy squirrel navels!

I've got the Hershey's bar with almonds all the
way down! Sprinkle dude ... can you give us any
more power?

Yes, but I'LL run out of sprinkles faster!

DO IT! If we don't speed up, that thing will run right over us!

MORE SPRINKLES!!!

sound of sprinkle machine sputtering

That's it! We're out of sprinkles! I've given everything I had for you, darling! But now there's just time for one sweet kiss before we die ...

(((•BING•))) UH ... THANKS ... BUT IT DOESN'T LOOK LIKE IT'S GOING TO KILL US.

sound of garbage truck extending
giant robot arms

What the sloth snot is it doing?

I AM GROOT!

It thinks we're **trash?** That's insulting!

sound of garbage truck arms picking up the FastTrash3000

Listen, you **stupid** trash truck, **we're not trash!!!**

sound of garbage truck roof opening

I'm serious. If you **dump** us in there, **I'm gonna be really mad.**

sound of garbage truck dumping

sound of furry woodland creature
getting really mad

sound of 347 pounds of stinking, disgusting
garbage getting dumped on furry
woodland creature, giant tree man
and totally awesome tape dispenser

sound of the *FastTrash3000* getting
dumped in and landing on furry
woodland creature

sound of furry woodland creature getting
really, really, really mad!

CAPTAIN'S LOG
10

STINKY PETE

CAPTAIN'S LOG!

This is **Captain Rocket**, former driver of the *FastTrash3000*.

We are currently in a pile of garbage in the back of a garbage truck that is being driven by an **insane** computer. Both of which I'm gonna personally **smash** into **itty-bitty pieces.**

Also, it smells bad! **Really bad!**

I AM GROOT!

It tastes good? What tastes good??? In the name of my granny's groundhog,

WHAT ARE YOU EATING?

I AM GROOT.

EW!

 (((•BING•))) EW!

EW!

 (((•BING•))) LISTEN! DO YOU HEAR THAT ...?

sound of faint talking

It sounds like somebody's up front in the driver's seat! But I thought these were all
self-driving vehicles.

((•BING•)) MY SENSORS INDICATE THAT YOU ARE CORRECT. THERE IS NO DRIVER UP THERE.

Then what the heck is going on? We gotta figure out some way to get up there. Maybe if I connect some—

I AM GROOT!

sound of giant tree man punching
a hole through the steel wall of the garbage
compartment into the driver's cab

That'll work.  **Let's go!**

Uh ... forgetting somebody?

No.

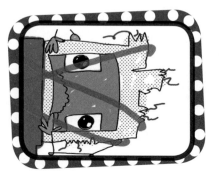 I'm still **taped** to the Dumpster!!!

And?

Don't leave me here! There's so much more joy I still want to sprinkle on the world! Please please please please take me with you!

Listen, sprinkle boy, you can take your joy and —

Sorry, Groot, even if we wanted him – which we don't – Veronica™ used her permanent weld-o-tape on him. He's stuck to that Dumpster forever! There's no way to take him with us!

(((•BING•))) ACTUALLY, THERE IS! I CAN DOWNLOAD HIS ELECTRONIC PERSONALITY AND STORE IT ON MY HARD DRIVE UNTIL WE FIND ANOTHER SPRINKLE MACHINE OR SOMETHING TO PUT HIM INTO.

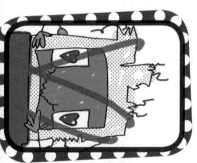

Oh, Veronica™! You're so wonderful! I will always lo—

(((•BING•))) DOWNLOAD COMPLETE!

Wait a minute!
He was just about to say something. He will always
WHAT?

I AM GROOT.

((•BING•)) NO! THAT IS NOT WHAT HE WAS GOING TO SAY. WE'RE JUST FRIENDS!!!!

I AM GROO-OO-OOOT...

sound of totally awesome tape dispenser blushing

sound of annoying giant tree man and annoying furry thing giggling because they think they are SO funny

All right, that's enough **mushy** stuff!
Let's go!

sound of furry woodland creature
and totally awesome tape dispenser
wriggling through the hole

sound of giant tree man wriggling
through the hole but getting stuck halfway

I told you not to **eat** that **garbage!**

I AM GROOT!

Well, there's not really room for you up here
anyway, dude. Just chill out for a minute ...

He
He   He   He   He
He   He

Well, land sakes! What do we have here? I didn't know I'd picked up **hitchhikers!**

((•BING•)) HITCHHIKING IS A DANGEROUS AND ILLEGAL ACTIVITY. WE WERE ACTUALLY RIDING IN A SPRINKLE-POWERED — OH, NEVER MIND.

I'm just tickled pink to have you folks on board! My name's Garbage Truck 4598P, but you can call me **Stinky Pete!**

Hey, Stinky Pete, we were wondering if —

Excuse me just one second, y'all!

sound of garbage truck swerving wildly, smashing into an ice cream truck, spinning out of control on slick ice-creamy street, then roaring off in a new direction at 150 miles per hour

Now what were y'all gonna ask me?

We were hoping you could give us a ride over to see the central computer.

You mean **Big Mama?** Sure, I'd be glad to. No problemo. Just let me check in with Big Mama first.

sound of radio static

What's that?

That's my CB! It's how us trucks and cars talk to each other ...
and to Big Mama!

(((•BING•))) CB RADIOS HAVE BEEN USED SINCE THE
LATE TWENTIETH CENTURY, WHEN TRUCKERS
ON EARTH USED THEM TO COMMUNICATE.

Breaker 1-9! This here's
Stinky Pete! Come
in, **BIG MAMA!**

THIS IS **BIG MAMA!** I'M PICKING
YOU UP TREETOP TALL AND WALL TO
WALL! COME BACK, **STINKY P!**

Big Mama, I just picked up some free riders — a tree, a
totally awesome tape dispenser and a really **ugly** squirrel!

ROGER THAT, STINKY PETE.

Hey! I ain't no squirrel!

Gonna need you to hush, squirrel!

sound of radio static

Big Mama, these folks want me to give 'em a ride over to see you.

THAT'S A **BIG** NEGATORY, SON.
YOU JUST GO AHEAD AND GIVE 'EM A
ONE-WAY RIDE TO FLY CITY.

The **Big Stink?**

YEAH, BUT SQUEEZE, PLEASE, COOL BREEZE, THEN POP THE BLOCKS IN THE HOT BOX.

10-4, Big Mama. Over.

Huh?

I said hush it up, squirrel.

Listen, pal, can you give us a ride or not?

You just sit tight, squirrel. I'll get you there in no time!

sound of garbage truck speeding up

Pssst ... Groot. I don't think I trust this trash truck ... and I definitely don't trust Big Mama.

I AM GROOT!

No, I got no clue what they were talking about. How about you, Veronica™?

 JUST A MOMENT. I'M DOWNLOADING THE DICTIONARY OF CB TALK AND TRUCKER SLANG. THEN I'LL TRY TO DECODE BIG MAMA'S INSTRUCTIONS.

sound of garbage truck screeching
around a corner, right into the back of
a minibike delivery truck

sound of garbage truck jolting up the
minibike truck's ramp and jumping over
an entire gridlocked intersection

sound of minibikes being knocked off
of minibike delivery truck and through the busted
window of H. F. Happy Tooth's candy shop

Okay, now I'm **REALLY** suspicious, because
we just passed Happy Tooth's again! We're headed the
wrong way! Where are you taking us, Stinky Pete?

I'm gonna keep that info on the down low, bro! Just sit back and
get all comfy, li'l squirrel!

sound of garbage truck making insanely sharp
turn, almost tipping over, then actually tipping
over, then barrel-rolling and coming back up
onto four wheels without ever
slowing down

sound of furry woodland creature almost
tipping over, then actually tipping over, then
barrel-rolling and landing on his face

Ugh ... I think I just chipped a fang ... Veronica™,
can you please, **FOR THE LOVE OF CAPYBARAS,**
hurry up and find out what's going on?!?!?!

 OKAY. DOWNLOAD COMPLETE. NOW
GIVE ME A SECOND TO DECODE THEIR
CONVERSATION.

sound of dramatic pause

(((●BING●))) # WE'RE ALL GOING TO DIE!!!!!!!!!!!!!!

Veronica™'s
CB TALK TRUCKER SLANG GUIDE!

Trucker Slang

`Yeah-huh, 10-4, roger that, copy that, uh-huh` = YES

`Negatory, naw, 86, scratch that, nuh-uh` = NO

`Put the hammer down, Stomp on the gas, Full throttle` = Go faster

`Jake brake` = A truck's engine brake, as opposed to the regular brakes

`Speed limit` = Obsolete term, no longer used

`Handle` = A nickname used to identify different CB users
(Examples: Big Mama, Stinky Pete, Lefty, Cranky Cobra, Kentucky Joe, Tennessee Williams, Rubber Duck, Tricky Woo, Lady Vivienne Von Vroom-Vroom, Rawhide, SuperToe)

`Fly City, the Big Stink` = Garbage dump

`Squeeze` = Trash compactor

`Hot box` = Trash incinerator = Big fire

`Haulin' fin` = Transporting sharks

`Bucktooth buggy` = Giant beaver carrier

`Bean machine` = Refried bean delivery vehicle

`He's on my donkey` = Someone is tailgating me

`Pop the blocks` = Drop off cargo

`Driving the devil` = Your engine is on fire

`Smoking the sky` = Your engine is on fire

`No, seriously, dude, your engine is on fire!!!!` = Your engine is on fire

`'Nuff said` = No further information should be required

`I am Groot` = I am Groot

`Good buddy, cool breeze, cap'n, hoss, son, honey, Larry` = Friendly terms similar to *dude*

Ten Codes

Commonly used phrases are assigned a ten code, such as 10-4, to speed up and/or simplify communication.

10-1 = Howdy!

10-2 = Listen to this!

10-3 = Would you shut up and listen?

10-4 = Okay

10-4-40-4 = Good luck!

10-5 = Speed up

10-6 = Slow down (rarely used)

10-7 = Destroy all life-forms

10-8 = Turn on your CB radio!

10-9 = Oh, wait, if your CB radio is off, then I guess you didn't hear me say 10-8

10-10 = Gonna stop at the truck stop and buy some origami paper

10-11 = Flat tire

10-12 = Dead battery

10-13 = Out of gas

10-14 = Out of Groot Smoothie

10-15 = How much tape do you need?

10-16 = A furry woodland creature needs to go to the bathroom

10-17 = Don't call me Shirley

10-18 = Who are you?

10-19 = Where are you?

10-20 = When do you get here?

10-21 = Oh! You're already here!

10-22 = Oopsie, we just crashed into each other!

10-37 = Feeling carsick

10-38 = Cracking the windows didn't help — I better pull over

10-39 = Blarffffffffffff!

10-42 = Don't panic

10-52 = Panic

10-66 = The Battle of Hastings

10-74 = I never got the point of all those math problems we had to do in school! I mean, how often do you have to divide something by a fraction? I mean, come on, it's ridiculous!

10-77 = Yeah, but I liked the book better than the movie

10-82 = Shark attack

10-99-A = I'm pulling over to get a gravy biscuit

10-99-B = I'm pulling over to get a fried bologna biscuit

10-99-C = I'm pulling over to get a ham biscuit with scrambled eggs and hash browns

10-99-D = It's none of your dang business what I'm having for breakfast! Get off my back, Larry!

CAPTAIN'S LOG
11

IT'S TRUCKER TALK, GOOD BUDDY!

CAPTAIN'S LOG!

This is **Captain Rocket**, former captain of
the **Rakk 'n' Ruin**, former pilot of the
FastTrash3000 and currently a passenger
in a speeding garbage truck —

sound of garbage truck rolling up
windows and locking doors

Er, make that a **PRISONER** of a speeding
garbage truck, which has been ordered to
squash us in a trash compactor and then burn us
in a trash furnace!

I AM GROOT!

Yeah, I know you don't like fire. I don't like it, either! I also don't like getting dumped, childnapped, compacted and/or called a squirrel! By the hairs of my black mask, I swear this:
I shall destr—

 MY MAP INDICATES THAT THE NEAREST TRASH COMPACTOR IS LESS THAN FIVE MILES AWAY.

I was in the middle of
swearing!!!

(((•BING•))) I WASN'T SURE HOW LONG YOU WERE GOING TO GO ON LIKE THAT. I THOUGHT YOU SHOULD KNOW THAT AT THE SPEED WE'RE TRAVELLING, WE'LL BE THERE IN ABOUT TWO MINUTES AND THIRTY-SEVEN SECONDS.

That gives me just enough time to play 'Eighteen Wheels and a Dozen Dumpsters' by Red Bovine!

sound of country music playing on radio

sound of Stinky Pete humming along

sound of giant tree man humming along

Why me?

What did I ever do
to deserve this?

 WOULD YOU LIKE ME TO READ A LIST OF THE GALACTIC FELONIES YOU'RE WANTED FOR?

Yes ... **but not right now.**

 THERE WOULDN'T BE TIME ANYWAY. IT'S A LONG LIST AND WE ONLY HAVE TWO MINUTES LEFT BEFORE WE GET TO THE TRASH COMPACTOR!

Don't worry, we'll never get there. Some kind of ice cream truck or something is going to smash into this garbage truck any second now!

(((•BING•))) ACTUALLY, IF YOU LOOK OUT THE WINDOW, YOU'LL NOTICE THAT ALL THE OTHER VEHICLES ARE PULLING OVER TO LET THE GARBAGE TRUCK THROUGH. REMEMBER, BIG MAMA IS CONTROLLING THEM ALL!

Capybara crud!!!! We can't buy a break on this crummy planet! All right, I guess I gotta fix this myself. Who's got a screwdriver? I'm gonna rip the brains out of this truck!

I AM GROOT!

What? You want to ask Stinky Pete a question first? What question could you possibly want to ask a criminally insane garbage truck with terrible taste in music?

I AM GROOT?

Actually, that **IS** a good question! Hey, Stinky! Can you tell us why Big Mama and all the cars and trucks have gone **crazy?**

Sure! The central computer was downloading an upgrade to the self-driving car programmes, right? Well, at the same time, some teenagers on Nova Prime were downloading a car chase movie marathon. Somehow the intergalactic **data streams got switched.** The teenagers ended up watching one hundred hours of really good drivers following all the safety rules. And the central computer got reprogrammed with:

Road Rage I, II and III
Mad Macks
The Fast and the Curious
18 Deadly Wheels
Night of the Driving Dead
Trucker and the Monkey
Monkey and the Trucker
Screeeeech!
Failure to Yield
HAUL-o-Ween
Kiss My Gas!

Guy with a Hat Driving a Car While This Lady Drives a Truck and a Different Guy Is a Cop or Something and They All Wreck a Lot
Truckin' 2: Electric Boogaloo
Speed Trap
Baby Behind the Wheel
The Hazzardous Dukes
WheelWolf 1, 2, 3 and 4
Splashzone 2: Revenge of the Narwhal

Excuse me one second, guys, while I run into this fruit stand for no real reason.

sound of truck smashing into fruit stand
for no real reason

Okay, where was I?

I think you were done.

sound of furry woodland creature
ripping the electronic brain out of the
truck's dashboard

Okay, that takes care of **that.**

I AM GROOT!!!!!

We're doing what?

I AM GROOT!!!!!!!!!!!

Heading straight for the trash compactor with
no way to steer **or stop?**
Holy wombat lips!

(((●BING●))) TWENTY SECONDS UNTIL SQUASH TIME!!!!

I AM GROOT!

Wait a second ... If we bail out, we'll just get run over by the next car that comes along. We gotta figure out a way to get control of this garbage truck!

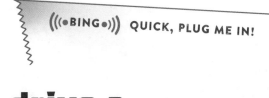

(((•BING•))) QUICK, PLUG ME IN!

You think you can **drive a garbage truck?**

(((•BING•))) PLUG ME IN AND FIND OUT, SQUIRREL!

CAPTAIN'S LOG

12

VERONICA™ TAKES THE WHEEL

CAPTAIN'S LOG!

This is **Captain Rocket**, of the ... well, captain of a **trash truck** right now.

Veronica™ is plugged into the dashboard in place of the truck's **(really annoying)** computer brain and is going to try to drive us safely to the central computer's computer centre.

((•BING•)) **VROOM-VROOM!** HOLD ON, BOYS, I'M GONNA TURN THIS RIG AROUND!

sound of tire-screeching, gear-jamming,
rubber-burning, precision-turning,
totally awesome driving

How the hamster did you get so **good**
at driving?

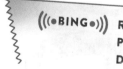 **REMEMBER ALL THOSE MOVIES THAT STINKY
PETE TOLD US ABOUT? THE ONES BIG MAMA
DOWNLOADED?**

You mean the movies that turned her from a safety
computer into a **murderous maniac?**

 (((•BING•))) YEP! I DOWNLOADED THEM ALL, TOO!

So that means –

(((•BING•))) IT MEANS YOU BETTER BUCKLE UP, GOOD BUDDY! BECAUSE THIS TRASH TRUCK HAS A LICENCE TO FLY! WE ARE HUGGSBURG BOUND AND DOWN! NEXT STOP: BIG MAMA'S HOUSE!

sound of radio static

YOU DIP-BLIPS DON'T THINK I'M
GONNA LET YOU ANYWHERE NEAR MY
COMPUTER CENTRE, DO YA?

(((•BING•))) LET ME HANDLE THIS.

(((•BING•))) AW, HEY, BIG MAMA. DON'T GET
YOUR DIALS TWISTED. WE JUST WANNA STOP
BY, SAY HI AND EAT SOME PIE.

SORRY, THE ONLY THING ON THE MENU
TODAY IS ... ROADKILL!!!

**ATTENTION ALL VEHICLES!
ATTENTION ALL VEHICLES!!** SCOPE
THAT TRASH TRUCK HEADING EASTBOUND
ON GRAVY MIX BOULEVARD? **KILL,
KILL, KILL!!!!!!!!!! DESTROY!
SMASH! CRASH!!!!**
DO YOU COPY ME?

Well, that sounds **bad**. I wonder how long it
will take before —

sound of compact car crashing
into our truck

$(((\bullet BING\bullet)))$ WE GET HIT BY SOMETHING BIG
ENOUGH TO –

sound of midsize sedan crashing
into our truck

Really damage us?

sound of SUV crashing into our truck

Groot, stick your head out and see if there's
anything **really big** coming.

I AM GROOT!

A bulldozer?

I AM GROOT!!!

And a dump truck??

I AM GROOT!!!!

And a cement mixer?

Sheesh! We better try to outrun them!! Step on the gas, Veronica™!

$((\bullet BING \bullet))$ I DO NOT HAVE FEET.

It's an expression! It was in your CB dictionary! It means go, and **go fast!**

$((\bullet BING \bullet))$ HEE-HEE!

This is no time for hilariosity!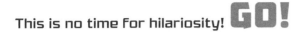

sound of totally awesome tape dispenser slamming on the brakes

 I CAN'T GO! THE WRECKAGE FROM THE FIRST THREE CARS IS BLOCKING OUR WAY! PLUS, THERE ARE TONS OF CARS COMING THIS WAY, TOO!

We need a plan!

 TIME TO THINK OF A PLAN BEFORE BEING CRUSHED TO DEATH: FORTY-THREE SECONDS.

Would you **stop that!!** It doesn't help me think any faster! In fact, all it does is waste time!

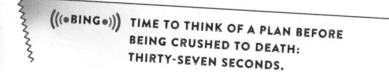 TIME TO THINK OF A PLAN BEFORE BEING CRUSHED TO DEATH: THIRTY-SEVEN SECONDS.

See what I mean??? It wasted ...
uh ... three minus seven ... borrow one from the
four ... six seconds!

(((•BING•))) TIME TO THINK OF A PLAN BEFORE BEING
CRUSH—

Never mind, I got it. **Big Mama** didn't realize
she was up against an **intellectuval!**

(((•BING•))) THAT'S NOT A WORD ...

Groot! You start throwing trash out of the
back at anything that gets too close!

I AM GROOT!

Nobody's going to
call you a litterbug ...
Just do it!

I'm gonna use this truck's
big trash-grabber arms to
clear us a path!

(((•BING•))) WHAT DO YOU NEED ME TO DO?

Can you do three things at once?

(((•BING•))) I CAN DO 256 THINGS AT ONCE!

Great! I just need **three** things:
1) Drive like the wind!
2) Reanalyze all those movies Big Mama watched
and see if you can figure out how to beat her.
3) Keep your eyes open for a rest stop!

Okay, everybody! **Do it!**

sound of giant tree man throwing the
FastTrash3000 at the dump truck, which
spins out of control, knocking the bulldozer
into the cement mixer, which tips over,
spilling cement all over the *FastTrash3000*,
creating a magnificent statue of the galaxy's
fastest dumpster, which schoolchildren
will visit for years to come

sound of furry woodland creature working the controls to make trash-grabber arms pick up smashed compact car and hurl it down the street like a bowling ball, knocking the other wreckage out of the way

Okay, Veronica™! **HIT THE GAS!!!**

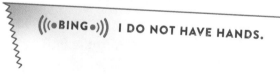

(((•BING•))) I DO NOT HAVE HANDS.

JUST g—

(((•BING•))) HEE-HEE!

sound of totally awesome tape dispenser totally hitting the gas and putting the hammer down

sound of garbage truck accelerating

Oh, yeah!!! We are **rolling now!**

sound of radio static

ROLLING RIGHT INTO MY TRAP, SQUIRREL! YOUR PLAN WASN'T BAD, BUT MY PLAN IS ALL GOOD, BABY!

First of all, **I'm not a squirrel**, and second of all ... **let's see what you got, Big Mama!**

CALLING ALL VEHICLES! REMEMBER THAT SCENE FROM *WHEELWOLF 4*? DO IT!

10-4, Big Mama!

sound of thousands and thousands
of engines revving

Okay, Veronica™ ... You've seen *WheelWolf 4*, right?

 *WHEELWOLF 4* TOTALLY ROCKED! SO MUCH
BETTER THAN *WHEELWOLF 3* AND WITH
BETTER ACTING THAN *WHEELWOLF 1 OR 2!*

I don't care about the acting! I want to know
what she's **ordering** them to do.

 THE END OF THE MOVIE FEATURED A GIANT
CRASH INVOLVING THREE HOT-SAUCE TANKER
TRUCKS, A FLEET OF SUSHI DELIVERY VANS
AND AN ORANGE DODGE CHARGER WITH
A FLAG PAINTED ON THE ROOF PULLING A
TRAILER FULL OF CRAYFISH.

sound of car horn playing the *1812 Overture* as Dodge Charger pulling trailer full of crayfish zooms towards garbage truck

Mmmmm! There are crayfish flying
everywhere!

Here come the hot sauce delivery tankers!
They're trying to **smash us** in a pincer move!
Throw it into reverse!

$((($\bullet$BING$\bullet$)))$ 10-4, GOOD BUDDY!

sound of garbage truck going into
reverse and making that annoying
beep, beep, beep sound

sound of hot-sauce trucks crashing
head-on into each other

OH, MY TAIL HAIR!
The hot sauce has spilled all over the crayfish!

(((•BING•))) HANG ON. I'M GONNA GET US OUT OF HERE BEFORE THOSE SUSHI VANS CLOSE IN ON US.

NO! Wait! Let me pick up some of those saucy crayfish!

sound of furry woodland creature trying to pick up saucy crayfish with garbage truck's robot arms

Would you **chill out** a minute? **This is tricky!**

sound of furry woodland
creature FAILING to pick
up any saucy crayfish
with garbage truck's
robot arms

Aw,
panda lips!

I'm just gonna
have to get down
there myself and
pick some up.

((●BING●)) **NOOOOO!**

I AM GROOT!

Yeah, I know the sushi vans are coming! I'm hoping to pick up some musubi when they get here!

(((•BING•)))

GROOT, LOOK! THE SUSHI VANS ARE ALL MONSTER TRUCKS! THEY'RE ENORMOUS!!!! THIS IS TOTALLY A TRAP! GRAB THE FURRY WOODLAND CREATURE AND LET'S GET OUT OF HERE!!!!

I AM GROOT!

sound of giant tree man grabbing furry
woodland creature

sound of furry woodland creature
squirming out of his grasp and using
some REALLY naughty words

(((•BING•))) **HURRY, GROOT!** WE'VE GOT TO GET
OUT OF HERE BEFORE IT'S TOO LATE!

sound of monster sushi delivery trucks
slamming into garbage truck

(((•BING•))) **IT'S TOO LATE!**

CAPTAIN'S LOG
13

ABANDON SHIP!

CAPTAIN'S LOG.

This is **Captain Rocket**, currently being —

> sound of another monster sushi delivery truck
> crashing into garbage truck

— held by Groot, who is —

> sound of another monster sushi delivery truck
> crashing into garbage truck

— in the back of a garbage truck on —

sound of another
monster sushi
delivery truck crashing
into –

Veronica™!
Isn't there anything we can do about all the crashing? I'm trying to record my Captain's Log here!

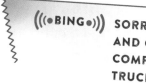

(((•BING•))) SORRY, ALL THE CRASHING AND SMASHING AND GENERAL CAR CRUNCHING HAS COMPLETELY WRECKED THE GARBAGE TRUCK. IT WON'T GO FORWARDS OR BACKWARDS, BUT IT WILL GO BOOM IN ABOUT THREE SECONDS!

ABANDON SHIP! Groot, grab

Veronica™ and jump!

I AM GROOT?

Jump as far away from this exploding garbage truck as you can, but make sure you land on another vehicle or we'll just get **run over!**

sound of giant tree man grabbing totally
awesome tape dispenser

I AM GROOT!

sound of giant tree man jumping while
carrying furry woodland creature and totally
awesome tape dispenser

sound of garbage truck exploding

sound of giant tree man landing with his left
foot on a frozen fish stick on wheels and his
right foot on a dog-slobber tank truck

I AM GROOT?

Gee, I wonder what the number one bev—

I AM GROOT!!!

Oh, **koala** pee-pee!! The frozen fish stick is turning left, and the slobber tanker is turning right!

sound of giant tree man doing a split!

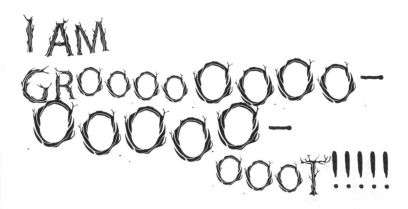

I AM GROOOOOOOOO-OOOOOO-OOOT!!!!!

Quick, Groot, jump onto that mobile karaoke machine!

sound of giant tree man jumping onto mobile karaoke machine

sound of giant tree man grabbing oversize
microphone and singing 'Let It Go'

You have got to be kidding me!
This is NOT the time!

sound of mobile karaoke machine
slamming into a needlessly large plastic
spork transporter

sound of giant tree man - with furry
woodland creature and totally awesome tape
dispenser clinging to his branches - being
hurled through the air

Tuck and roll, Groot!
Tuck and roll!!!!

sound of giant tree man tucking and rolling, then bouncing off a Gather the Magicking card game truck and landing on a bookmobile like a skateboarder

Veronica™, see if you can take control of this bookmobile!

sound of totally awesome tape dispenser going into Ninja Mode and smashing through the windshield

Howdy! Would you like to check out a book? We have the latest novel from Tom Angleberger. It's simply —
BZZZZZRTTTTTT-blip-squuuuuuu—pfft.

sound of totally awesome tape dispenser ripping out the truck's computer brain

 ((•BING•)) **THAT'S A BIG 10-4**, ROCKET! I'M DRIVING THIS BOOKMOBILE NOW!

Look out for that tractor-trailer full of
Porta-Potties!!!

Wait a minute ... Don't look out for it!
Go straight for it.

Here, Groot, you handle the Captain's Log for a minute. I've got some business to take care of.

CAPTAIN'S LOG

14

BUSINESS

I AM GROOT.

(((•BING•))) I AGREE 100 PER CENT! THOSE PORTA-POTTIES ARE DEFINITELY ANOTHER TRAP!

I AM GROOT!

(((•BING•))) YEP. OH, YEAH, LOOK AT THAT. EWWW ... THAT'S BAD.

I AM GROOT!!!!!!!

sound of giant tree man drawing a scene
of unspeakable mayhem, horror, destruction
and Porta-Potties.

CAPTAIN'S LOG

15

OVERDUE

CAPTAIN'S LOG!

This is **Captain Rocket**, currently captain of the
HappyHappyFunFun Regional Library bookmobile.

And we are seriously **OVERDUE** at
Big Mama's island fortress.

                    awkward silence

Get it? **OVERDUE?**

                    awkward silence

We're in a library bookmobile and we're

OVERD—LOOK OUT! We're

headed right for that truckload of White
Knight–brand oversize chess pieces!

((•BING•)) I KNOW!

sound of totally awesome tape dispenser
gunning the engine

((•BING•)) PURPLE QUEEN TAKES WHITE KNIGHT ...

sound of bookmobile totally smashing the snot
out of the chess piece truck

((•BING•)) CHECKMATE, CHUMP!

This is Captain Rocket again. I think I forgot to mention that Veronica™, who is driving the bookmobile, seems to have gone a little —

OH, MY MUSKRAT!!!!

Look out for that mail truck!

sound of bookmobile totally running mail truck
off the road and into a post office

(((•BING•))) **RETURN TO SENDER!**

Undies Express van coming in fast!

(((•BING•))) DON'T GET YOUR PANTIES IN A TWIST!

sound of bookmobile ramming the
back of the van

sound of underwear flying everywhere

(((•BING•))) **YEEEE-HAW!!!!**
WE TOTALLY LEFT A SKID MARK ON THAT UNDERWEAR TRUCK!

Yeah, but all that underwear got stuck in Groot's branches! Plus, riding on top of this thing is messing up my fur. Don't you think maybe it's time to turn off **Insane Trucker Mode** and maybe drive a little more sensibly?

(((•BING•))) NEGATORY.

Remember when I asked you to analyze all those movies? Do you think maybe they've affected your **brain**, too?

(((•BING•))) NOT AT ALL. I'M STILL COMPLETELY SANE AND READY TO DISPENSE AS MUCH TAPE AS YOU NEED. NOW ... ARE YOU BOYS READY TO JUMP? BECAUSE I THINK I SEE WHAT I'VE BEEN LOOKING FOR!

I AM GROOT?

(((•BING•))) IT'S THAT SPORTS CAR UP AHEAD!

You mean the one that's headed straight at us at **300 miles an hour?**

(((•BING•))) 308 MILES PER HOUR, ACTUALLY.

(((•BING•))) READY ...

(((•BING•))) **JUMP!**

sound of giant tree man, furry woodland
creature and totally awesome tape dispenser
jumping from the bookmobile

sound of bookmobile crashing through
the front wall of the HappyHappyFunFun
Regional Library

sound of giant tree man, furry woodland
creature and totally awesome tape
dispenser landing in the deluxe leather seats
of a Porshagini 9000b convertible

SWEET! THIS IS THE 9000B MODEL! MUCH FASTER THAN THE 9000A. WE ARE GOING TO BURN SOME RUBBER NOW!!

sound of rubber burning

I AM GROOT?

I don't know, either, buddy! I think she's gone a little **nuts!**

HEY, THAT'S A PERFECT CB NICKNAME! LITTLE NUT!

 BREAKER 1-9, ATTENTION ALL VEHICLES! THIS HERE'S LITTLE NUT AND I AM THE QUEEN OF THE ROAD, THE EMPRESS OF THE HIGHWAYS AND THE BADDEST TAPE DISPENSER YOU EVER SAW! SO JUST PULL OVER AND LET ME THROUGH!

THIS IS **BIG MAMA**, CALLING LITTLE NUT! YOU AIN'T SEEN **NOTHING** YET, HONEY.

 **BRING IT ON, BIG MAMA!**

YOU ASKED FOR IT, **ROADKILL!**

CALLING ALL UNITS, CALLING ALL UNITS. **START THE 10-82!** I REPEAT, **START THE 10-82!**

Uh, I forgot. What's a 10-82?

I AM GROOT!

I was afraid you were gonna say that.

CAPTAIN'S LOG

16

10-82

CAPTAIN'S LOG!

This is **Captain Rocket**, currently captain of a **Porshagini 9000**.

(((•BING•))) IT'S A PORSHAGINI 9000B.

Uh, yeah ... So, we're currently dealing with a 10-82. Also known as a ...

SHARK ATTACK !!!!!!!!!!!

SLOSH

SCREECH

sound of mobile shark tanks closing in

sound of shark jaws chomping

Just out of curiosity, I wonder what kind of sharks these are.

 **(((•BING•)))** MY DNA ANALYSIS SUGGESTS THAT THEY ARE GIANT RACCOON-EATING SHARKS.

Whew! They only eat
giant raccoons!

(((•BING•))) NO, ACTUALLY, THE WORD *GIANT* APPLIES TO THE SIZE OF THE SHARKS. THEY EAT ALL SIZES OF RACCOON.

Well, it's still not a problem, because
I ain't a raccoon!

I AM GROOT!

What do you mean, I smell like one? Dude,
that's hurtful!

sound of shark lunging out of tank
directly at furry woodland creature who smells
like the shark's favourite food

Muskrat nostrils!!!!!!! I'm a
sitting duck in this convertible!

(((•BING•))) I THOUGHT YOU WERE A RACCOON?

Yummy, I love raccoon!

I AM GROOT!

**sound of giant tree man catching shark
at last possible second**

Thanks, Groot!

**sound of shark tank water sloshing
into convertible**

**sound of giant tree man soaking up water and
growing bigger and bigger**

I AM
GROOOOOOOOOT!!!!!!!

sound of really, really giant tree man
throwing shark at closest mobile shark tank,
which bursts, spilling even more water into the
Porshagini 9000b

sound of giant tree man growing so ridiculously big that he barely fits in the car and the tape dispenser and furry woodland creature are totally getting smooshed

We're gonna need a bigger car.

((•BING•)) I'VE GOT A BETTER IDEA.

What is it?

((•BING•)) IT'S A SURPRISE!

Groot **hates** surprises.

((•BING•)) OH, ALL RIGHT, I'M GOING TO CRASH INTO THAT FIRE HYDRANT AT 300 MILES PER HOUR.

I'm not sure that's such a great —

sound of Porshagini 9000b crashing into fire
hydrant at 300 miles an hour

sound of Porshagini 9000b
flipping into the air

sound of really giant tree man, furry
woodland creature and totally awesome
tape dispenser falling out of
Porshagini 9000b

sound of tape dispenser landing in the cab of
a passing lumber truck that has one of those
awesome cranes for delivering lumber

sound of really giant tree man landing
flat on the bed of the passing lumber
truck that has one of those awesome
cranes for delivering lumber

sound of furry woodland creature landing in
the jaws of a giant raccoon-eating shark

That was the **worst plan ever**,
Li'l Nut!!!!!!!!

I AM GROOT!

sound of Groot punching shark

sound of shark spitting out furry woodland creature

sound of lumber truck's crane claw grabbing woodland creature by the tail

Whew! That was close! And **stinky**. Thanks, guys!

I AM GROOT!

 ((•BING•)) 10-4, GOOD BUDDY!

So, Veronica™, are you operating the crane?

All right then ... swing me
around some more! I'm ready to

make some sushi!

I AM GROOT!

(((●BING●))) ME TOO!

sound of crane swinging furry
woodland creature around

sound of furry woodland creature
punching sharks in the face

sound of giant tree man punching and
kicking sharks, trucks, vans, cars and
anything else that gets too close

sound of totally awesome tape dispenser
driving in a totally awesome way

((•BING•)) **YEE-HAW!** I'M LARGE AND IN CHARGE NOW, BOYS! THIS LUMBER TRUCK IS JACKED UP AND I'M ABOUT TO HAMMER DOWN! NOTHING CAN STOP US NOW!!!

THAT'S WHAT YOU THINK!

sound of loudest engine ever

sound of loudest engine ever coming
up behind us FAST!

NO! NO! **IT CAN'T BE!!!!!!**

((•BING•))

WHAT IS IT? MY SENSORS INDICATE THAT IT'S SOME SORT OF ZOO VEHICLE, BUT I CAN'T GET A DNA READING ON THE ANIMAL YET ...

It's ... it's ... an insanely large

BEAVER!

I AM
GROOOOOOOOOT!!!!!!!!

CAPTAIN'S LOG

17

INSANELY LARGE
BEAVER ATTACK!!!!

CAPTAIN'S LOG!

This is **Captain Rocket**, and we are in deep doo-doo.

There is an **insanely large beaver truck** behind us, and it's carrying an **insanely large beaver**, which is trying to take an **insanely large bite** out of Groot with its **insanely large teeth!**

I AM GROOOOOOT!!!!!!!

I know, buddy, I know! I'm trying to think
of something!

I AM GROOT???

NO! I can't think of anything!

How about you, Veronica™?

((•BING•)) Y'ALL HANG TIGHT. I GOT THIS ...

((•BING•)) BREAKER 1-9, THIS IS LITTLE NUT
CALLING HAPPY TOOTH!

This here's
Happy Tooth.
You ready for
us, Little Nut?

((•BING•)) COME ON!

Robo-fairies, start your engines ... and start your Battle Modes ... WE RIDE!!!!

sound of minibike ridden by robotic tooth
wearing a monocle

sound of many minibikes ridden
by bloodthirsty robo-tooth fairies in
Battle Mode

sound of one minibike ridden by
cute lizard-like alien child

KILL KILL KILL!!!!

Actually, adorable lizard-like alien child, we don't have to kill the beaver. We're just going to squirt some of this delicious high-fructose corn syrup on his teeth! You may fire when ready, robo-fairies!

sound of bloodthirsty robo-fairies spraying syrup on beaver teeth

sound of tooth decay beginning

NOOOOO!!!!

Sorry, Big Mama, I've got to go floss! Proper dental care is very important to me.

sound of insanely large beaver truck
making a U-turn and carrying insanely
large beaver off into the sunset

DING-DANG!

Great job, Happy Tooth!!!

You got it, groundhog! I just wish Bobby
Sprinkles Jr. was here to see it.

We'll tell him all about it later. Right now we've got
a date with Big Mama! And now there's **nothing
that can stop us!**

(((•BING•))) UNFORTUNATELY, YOU ARE RIGHT! ONE OF THE SHARKS BIT THROUGH THE BRAKE LINES! WE CANNOT STOP AND ...

sound of dramatic pause

(((•BING•))) ... WE'RE HEADED STRAIGHT FOR THE OCEAN!

Can't we jump the gap between the mainland and Big Mama's island fortress?

(((•BING•))) NO. IT'S TOO FAR! WE'D LAND RIGHT IN SHARK-INFESTED WATERS!

sound of really dramatic pause

Don't worry. I got a plan! Groot, hand me those underpants!

CAPTAIN'S LOG
18

THE PLAN

CAPTAIN'S LOG!

This is **Captain Rocket**. We're on the back of a lumber truck with **no brakes** going **240 miles per hour** towards a mile-high sea cliff. So ... can't really talk now. Kinda busy getting the plan together.

END OF THE ROAD

1 MILE

((•BING•)) DID I MENTION THAT THERE ARE MORE SHARKS IN THE OCEAN?

GIANT RACCOON-EATING SHARKS

INSANELY LARGE MERBEAVER

MORE SHARKS!

sound of furry woodland creature taking
apart logging crane

(((•BING•))) I MEAN A LOT MORE SHARKS!

sound of really, really giant tree man
tying underpants together

(((•BING•))) AND INSANELY LARGE **MERBEAVERS!**

sound of furry woodland creature
using the tied-together underpants and
various parts of the logging crane to
create giant slingshot

(((•BING•))) ALSO, SALT WATER MAY DAMAGE MY SPARKLY
EXTERIOR, CORRODE MY WIRING AND VOID
MY WARRANTY!

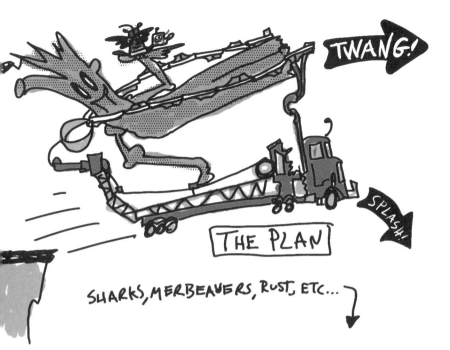

TWANG!

SPLASH!

THE PLAN

SHARKS, MERBEAVERS, RUST, ETC...

sound of giant tree man loading
himself into giant slingshot

sound of totally awesome tape dispenser
trying to figure out what the odds are of
this plan actually working

sound of furry woodland creature clearing
throat and posing majestically

Once more unto the breach, dear Fr—

(((•BING•))) EXCUSE ME.

Why do you always **interrupt** when I'm quoting Shakespeare?

(((•BING•))) BECAUSE MY CALCULATIONS SHOW THAT INSTEAD OF GOING ONCE MORE UNTO THE BREACH, WE'RE ABOUT TO GO INTO THE OCEAN!

But we made this
awesome slingshot!

(((•BING•))) NOT ONLY IS SLINGSHOTTING A TAPE DISPENSER OVER SHARK-AND-MERBEAVER-INFESTED WATERS NOT AN APPROVED USE ... BUT IT WON'T WORK.

What if I really, **really, really** want it to work?

((•BING•)) I'M SORRY, NO. GROOT IS JUST TOO BIG! HE WEIGHS THIRTY-SEVEN TONS RIGHT NOW. THE SLINGSHOT IS BARELY GOING TO SHOOT HIM OVER THE HOOD OF THE TRUCK.

I AM GROOT!

Groot says he can **scale down!** How small do you need him?

((•BING•)) RECALCULATING ...

I don't mean to rush you, but the edge of the cliff is coming up **fast.**

((•BING•)) RECALCULATING ...

Okay, don't panic, but we just went over the edge of the cliff and are **plunging** straight for the ocean. How small do you need Groot to be?!

 OKAY, YOU SEE THAT LITTLE TWIG STICKING OUT OF GROOT'S FOREHEAD?

Yes.

(((•BING•))) EXACTLY THAT SMALL.

Can you do that, Groot?

I AM GROOT!

sound of twig snapping

sound of furry woodland creature
grabbing twig

sound of furry woodland creature grabbing
totally awesome tape dispenser

Once more unto the breach!
Release the underwear!!!

sound of a hundred pairs of
underwear twanging

sound of tiny tree man, furry woodland creature and totally awesome tape dispenser soaring high above the ocean, directly towards Big Mama's island fortress

sound of logging truck crashing into ocean

Don't look, Groot! Merbeavers are already chewing on your old body. Ew, gross, they just ate your head ... Wait a minute! Your legs just kicked a merbeaver in the face! And another one! Now your legs are swimming away! They're free!!! Keep swimming, Groot legs! Keep swimming!!!!!

I AM GROOT...

Yeah, I can understand how you feel. I'd feel the same way if I was watching my head get eaten by merbeavers while my legs swam away.

(((•BING•))) SORRY TO INTERRUPT, BUT WE ARE PASSING DIRECTLY OVER BIG MAMA'S ISLAND FORTRESS.

Hmmm ... I think we're gonna **need some tape.**

(((•BING•))) HOW MUCH TAPE DO YOU NEED?

Exactly enough to make a parachute that will slow us down and bring us in for **an easy landing** in Big Mama's island fortress.

(((•BING•))) HERE YOU GO!

sound of totally awesome tape
dispenser dispensing tape

sound of furry woodland creature using
it to make a steerable parachute with
special pouches for the tiny tree man and
the totally awesome tape dispenser

sound of tiny tree man, furry woodland
creature and totally awesome tape dispenser
floating gently down for an easy landing in
Big Mama's island fortress

sound of awkward silence

Wow, this is really taking

a
long
time.

sound of awkward silence

How you doing, Groot?

I AM GROOT.

(((•BING•))) AW! HE'S SO CUTE!!!

I AM GROOT!!!!!!

sound of awkward silence

I almost hate to ask, but how long until impact?

(((•BING•))) IMPACT, WHICH WILL ACTUALLY BE A GENTLE LANDING, WILL OCCUR IN TWELVE MINUTES AND THIRTY-SEVEN SECONDS.

Okay, thanks.

I AM GROOT.

 **SURE! I'D BE GLAD TO PLAY SOME MUSIC! HOW ABOUT SOME MID-1970S DISCO?**

NO!!!!! Anything but that!!!!!

sound of mid-1970s disco

sound of totally adorable tiny
tree man dancing! OMG he's
soooooooo cute!!!!!!!!!!!!!!!!

CAPTAIN'S LOG
19

BIG MAMA!

This is **Captain Rocket**, currently captain of —
well, nothing much, actually.

We've just landed inside Big Mama's fortress.

I'm just gonna come right out and say it:
the fortress stinks. I mean,
this is a fortress?

(((•BING•))) ACTUALLY, THIS IS THE CENTRAL COMPUTER'S
COMPUTER CENTRE. FROM HERE, THE CENTRAL
COMPUTER – A.K.A. BIG MAMA – CONTROLS
EVERY VEHICLE ON THE PLANET.

Great, now let's **bust in** and finish the job by
smashing Big Mama to bits and bytes!

I AM GROOT.

I agree, dude! That took all the fun out of busting in. Oh, well, let's just **WALK in** and finish the job.

sound of furry woodland creature
carrying tiny dancing tree man and
totally awesome tape dispenser into the
central computer's computer centre.

HOWDY, BOYS! HOWDY, LITTLE NUT!

Who said that?

AW, HONEY, IT'S ME, BIG MAMA!

All I see is an old laptop computer hooked up to a radio with a coat hanger sticking out of it.

THAT'S ME!!!

(whispering) Uh, should I smash it?

 (((•BING•))) (volume: 1) NO, IF YOU DO THAT THE LIZARD-LIKE ALIEN PEOPLE WILL BE STUCK WITH MILLIONS OF CARS AND TRUCKS THAT WON'T RUN AT ALL. LET ME TRY TO FIX HER ...

FIX ME? NO THANKS! I NEVER WANT TO GO BACK TO BEING A STUPID OLD SAFETY MONITOR AGAIN! DRIVING SENSIBLY! OBEYING THE SPEED LIMITS! GIVING WAY TO PEDESTRIANS! **BORING!!!!**

((•BING•)) BUT, BIG MAMA, YOU'VE TURNED THIS WHOLE PLANET INTO A CRAZY NEVER-ENDING CAR CHASE!

YEAH! THAT WAS FUN, WASN'T IT? WANT TO PLAY AGAIN?

PLAY AGAIN????? Are you **crazy????**

YEP. I SURE AM! I GOT HOT-ROD FEVER! TRUCKIN' MADNESS! ROAD RAGE! I'M FAST! AND I'M FURIOUS! I GOT A NEED FOR SPEED!

HEY, LISTEN, Y'ALL ... DID YOU KNOW I ALSO CONTROL ALL THE AEROPLANES, HELICOPTERS, BOATS, SUBMARINES AND MONSTER-FIGHTING ROBOTS ON THE PLANET, TOO? AND THEY'RE ALL HEADED THIS WAY RIGHT NOW TO SMASH AND CRASH WITH YOU!

Gee, that does sound like Fun!!!

(((●BING●))) CAN I CONTROL ONE OF THE MONSTER-FIGHTING ROBOTS? I'VE ALWAYS WANTED TO KARATE CHOP ROBO-DINOSAURS AND KNOCK OVER BUILDINGS AND STUFF!

I GOT ROAD RAGE!

OH, YEAH!!!! IT'S GONNA BE BETTER THAN THE END OF *SPLASHZONE 2: REVENGE OF THE NARWHAL!!!!* FIRST THE HELICOPTERS ARE GOING TO DROP THE TURBO SUBS ON YOUR—ZZZRRRRRPL.

What just happened?

I AM GROOT.

You pulled the plug?

I AM GROOT.

Aw, man!

I AM GROOT.

(((•BING•))) AW, MAN!

I AM GROOT.

But, dude ... turbo subs!

I AM GROOOOOOOT!

All right, all right ... Veronica™, will you install the proper software on the central computer so the cars stop acting **crazy** and the lizard-like alien people can come out of the caves and this planet can go back to being **happy-happy-fun-fun** again?

(((•BING•))) YEAH, I GUESS ... I NEVER GET TO HAVE ANY FUN ... JUST WANTED TO DRIVE A BIG ROBOT ... GEE WHIZ ...

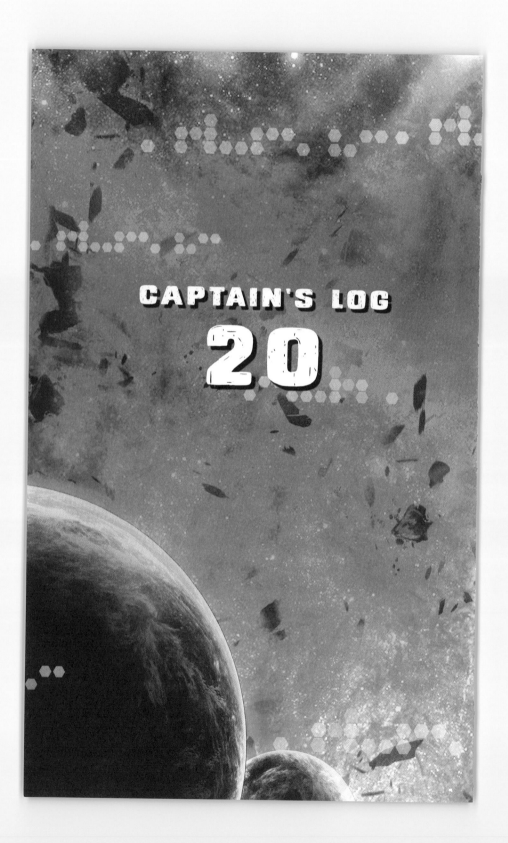

CAPTAIN'S LOG

20

RETURN OF THE BOBBY

Captain's Log.

This is **Captain Rocket!**

Wow, the central computer's computer centre has some great vending machines! Also a first-aid kit! And an office plant.

So I ate some **Funyuns**, put on, like, **fifty** Band-Aids and repotted Groot while Veronica™ has been reprogramming the central computer.

(((●BING●))) I JUST FINISHED! LET'S SEE IF IT WORKS ...

Hey, everybody! It's me, Bobby Sprinkles Jr.! Let's get this planet back in shape ... but let's do it safely and with smiles! Tow trucks, get busy, but remember, safety first! All buses, please stop at the nearest cave to pick up some lizard-like alien people, and then drive them carefully to their homes! All construction vehicles, please drive very carefully to the nearest disaster area and . . .

You made **Bobby Sprinkles Jr.** the new central computer?

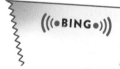 **(((•BING•)))** YES! I ALSO DOWNLOADED ALL THIRTY-FOUR SEASONS OF *TIMMY THE HAPPY HELPFUL HONDA.* SO NOW HE – AND EVERY VEHICLE ON THE PLANET – IS OBSESSED WITH SAFETY ... AND SMILES.

Sounds awful ... I almost miss Big Mama. In fact ... **what happened** to Big Mama?

(((•BING•))) I UPLOADED HER TO HAPPYHAPPYFUNFUN'S BIGGEST TV NETWORK. SHE'S IN CHARGE OF ALL PROGRAMMING NOW.

Well, I guess President Dee-Dee won't think TV's **boring** anymore. Sounds like a happy ending for everybody.

(((•BING•))) YOU MEAN A **HAPPY-HAPPY-FUN-FUN** ENDING!!!!

That reminds me ... LET'S GET THE MONKEYBUTT OFF THIS PLANET BEFORE THE HUGGING STARTS!!!!

CAPTAIN'S LOG
21

THE HUGGING

Captain's Log.

This is **Captain Rocket** of the spaceship
Rakk 'n' Ruin.

Yes, we are **FINALLY** back on the ship! **First** we
had to wait for a really happy crane to pull it out of
the rubble.

Then we had to wait for a really happy fuel truck to fill it up with gas.

Then we had to wait while H. F. Happy Tooth and his robo-fairies sang us a song, and that made Groot dance some more.

Yeah, we get that. Enough.

Then we had to wait while Happy Tooth gave us some coupons. And then the robo-fairies tried to

hug us.

Then we had to wait for the really happy lizard-like alien people to tell us how really happy they are to get out of the caves. And then they tried to

hug us.

Then we had to wait while President Dina the Wonder Lizard made a speech about how the new happy cars are even happier than the old cars, which were just safe and not always happy. And then she tried to **hug us.**

Then that adorable lizard-like alien child said something.

((•BING•)) SHE SAID, 'ME WUV SQWIRREL'.

And then she tried to **hug me!!!**

Thankfully, that **nightmare** is all over now. Veronica™, please plug into the controls and get the *Rakk 'n' Ruin* ready for **takeoff.**

((•BING•)) DID YOU WANT TO QUOTE SHAKESPEARE SOME MORE?

Naw, let's just get **out of here!**

((•BING•)) 10-4, GOOD BUDDY!

Wait a minute! Veronica™, you deleted all those crazy driving movies from your memory, right? You're back to being safe and sensible, right?

((•BING•)) THERE'S ONLY ONE WAY TO FIND OUT! NOW BUCKLE UP, BOYS, 'CAUSE I'M ABOUT TO PUT THE HAMMER DOWN!

YEEEE-HAW!!!

sound of the *Rakk 'n' Ruin* blasting off in a reckless and unapproved manner

AAAAAAAH!

FROM **BIG MAMA**, THE TV
PRODUCER WHO BROUGHT YOU
AN ENTIRE PLANETLOAD OF ROAD
RAGE AND MOTORIZED MAYHEM,
COMES THE HOTTEST NEW TV
SHOW IN THE HISTORY OF TV!!!!!

THESE TWO TREE COPS CAN WALK, DRIVE
AND CATCH EVEN THE BADDEST BAD GUYS ...
BUT CAN THEY LEARN TO GET ALONG?

HOW TO DRAW G-ROOT

LOOP

1

SQUIGGLES

2

BUMP